Daughter

Daughter

by Ishbel Moore

Kids Can Press

Kids Can Press acknowledges the financial support of the Ontario Arts
Council, the Canada Council for the Arts and the Government of Canada,
through the BPIDP, for our publishing activity.

Published in Canada by
Kids Can Press Ltd.
29 Birch Avenue
Toronto, ON M4V 1E2

Published in the U.S. by
Kids Can Press Ltd.
2250 Military Road
Tonawanda, NY 14150

www.kidscanpress.com

Edited by Charis Wahl
Interior designed by Karen Birkemoe
Printed and bound in Canada

CM 99 0 9 8 7 6 5 4 3 2 1
CM PA 99 0 9 8 7 6 5 4 3 2

Canadian Cataloguing in Publication Data

Moore, Ishbel L. (Ishbel Lindsay), 1954–
    Daughter

ISBN 1-55074-535-2 (bound)   ISBN 1-55074-537-9 (pbk.)

I. Title.

PS8576.06141D38 1999   jC813'.54   C99-930909-9
PZ7.M66Da 1999

Kids Can Press is a Nelvana company

To Deena, who shared and remembers
our bright days of youth and who
always told me I could do it.

ACKNOWLEDGMENTS

Thanks to Dr. R.A. and the staff of KMC;
to my teen readers Tara, Edythe, Erica, Katie and Tia
for their critiques of the original manuscript;
and to the many wonderful people who helped me
better understand Alzheimer disease through their
experiences. I'd also like to acknowledge Charis Wahl
for helping me find the way through the maze. — IM

Chapter One

"Mom! What are you doing? Get down from there!"

I slam the door, drop my back-pack and rush across the living room.

One of Mom's feet is curled over the tenth floor balcony railing, the other is tiptoe on the top of the small stepladder. One hand is around the chain of the empty hanging basket. The screw that holds the basket is coming loose from its plastic socket in the ceiling. I can see the crumbling white dust.

"Mom!" I shout up at her, my fingers doing little dances around her ankles as she sways. "Get down! Please, please, get down."

She stares blankly. For a split second, I follow her gaze over the treetops to where the Red River winds a white ribbon of frozen water under the Chief Peguis Trail Bridge.

A sudden gust of cold February wind grabs at her long blonde hair, and she sways even more. I slap my hands tightly over my mouth. If I startle her, she might slip. I think I'm going to be sick.

The phone rings. I can't leave her. Another ring.

Mom twirls on the balls of her feet and leaps gracefully to the snow-packed floor of the balcony. She sends me an innocent smile and heads for the phone. I struggle to bring my breathing back to normal as I follow, locking the balcony doors behind me. I stare at the patches of ice along the metal tracks and wonder how she managed to open the sliding doors in the first place.

"Hello. Marianne speaking," she says, her voice light and controlled. "Yes, Mr. Bartlet, I'm fine. No, no, you're not bothering me. I was just enjoying the view."

I study her carefully as she talks. What's going on? She's my old mom, the one who teaches grade five, the one who can be calm and sparkling at the same time, the one who is always in control. The person on the edge of the balcony had definitely not been in control.

Mom lowers herself into one of the pink wingback chairs and crosses her legs. "Thank you for being so understanding, Mr. Bartlet. Not all principals would be, I'm sure. Yes, no doubt you are right, Mr. Bart— I mean Tom. It's likely just stress. Yes, sir. Tom. I'll take care of myself. Good-bye."

She drops the receiver into the cradle as if it was covered in something unpleasant and wipes her hands across the front of her white tracksuit. Then, as if suddenly remembering I exist, she comes over and hugs me.

"Sylvie, you're home. Is it that late? What time is it anyway?" She squints at the dome clock on the piano.

"Three-thirty," I answer, trying not to look at the pile of music books. I won't think about my grade six conservatory exam coming up. "What were you doing on the balcony just now?"

"What's that, Sylvie?"

She's stalling.

"What were you doing on the balcony?"

"Like I told Mr. Bartlet. I mean, Tom. I'm to call him Tom even though he's only been at our school since, since, gosh ..." She stops running water into the kettle. "Since Christmas."

"You always call him Tom. You said he told the staff to call him Tom on his very first day."

"Oh," she says, going as pink as the living room chairs. "Well, yes, I guess I just forgot." She shrugs. "Well, like I told Tom, I was enjoying the view."

"Yeah, right!" I glare at her. "You were gonna jump." I don't feel sick anymore. Now I'm shaking with anger, frustration.

"Don't be silly. Really, Sylvie. I wanted to see the river and had to get up higher."

"It sure didn't look like that to me. You scared me out of my friggin' boots."

"Sylvie," she gasps, and I know she's going to change the subject from her nearly jumping from the tenth floor to my nearly swearing. She changes the subject, all right. "You've tracked snow all over the carpet! Get over to the door and take those boots off. Now!"

"Mom," I moan, "forget about the stupid carpet."

"I will not. Boots off."

"This is serious, Mom," I growl, and prepare to set my boots neatly in the hall closet. Shocked, I stare at the mess on the closet floor. Mom's brown leather boots have been carelessly thrown in, leaving running shoes and sandals soles up or sideways. She's never done that before. Everything's always been lined up in pairs. Should I straighten them for her? Not when she's in this kind of mood. But I straighten them anyway – for me.

"Yes, it is serious," she says. "I spend a lot of time keeping this place clean. I know it's not very fancy, but it's clean."

A click startles me – the sound of a stove element being turned on. That kick-starts my brain. I fly into the kitchen and snatch the kettle off the heat. The back element is at max.

"What are you doing!" I scream. "You don't put this on the stove. It plugs in, remember? Electric!" I shake the kettle, spilling water on the element, causing little spots of hissing. I wave the cord in her startled face. "This here thing is called a plug. It goes in this funny-looking holey bit in the wall called a socket."

She brushes by me and steps down into the sunken living room. "Plug it in and shut up. I've had a bad day."

"*You've* had a bad day!" Before I can launch into the finer points of coming home to a crazy mother, she interrupts.

"I had to leave school today. Actually, I was asked to leave and told to get myself together." She straightens the doily under the crystal candy dish filled with yogurt-covered raisins. "Put the kettle down if you're not going to plug it in. You're getting water all over."

I plug in the kettle and drop onto a kitchen chair.

She sighs. "Tom thinks I should see a doctor."

"Good idea. You *were* gonna jump."

"Cut it out," she snaps. "I was not going to jump. I was fixing the hanging basket."

"And enjoying the view," I add, dripping sarcasm.

"Don't get smart with me, Sylvie. Try a bit of sympathy now and then."

I can't stand it anymore. If she says she wasn't going to jump, then fine, who am I to argue? Besides, right now, if she climbed up to enjoy the view, I might just give her a push. I shake my head to get that thought out of my brain.

"Don't you sigh and shake your head like that, miss!" she shouts. "You don't know the half of it."

"Maybe I don't want to know." I yank out the plug of the boiling kettle and march to the closet. I stuff my feet into my boots, grab my jacket and open the door.

I turn to see her, white faced and stricken, in her smudged tracksuit and uncombed hair. I wait for my good side to take over. It might hug her and give her the sympathy she asks for. Nothing happens. I wait another moment, to give her a chance to say something, anything, to stop me from stomping out. Nothing!

The door slams behind me as I run down the apartment building's long hallway.

I stand in the empty elevator, blow my nose and dab my eyes. In the mirror tiles, my reflection looks very grumpy. I stare back with gloomy gray eyes at my thick black hair that hangs to below my ears. A tear runs down my cheek. I look so much like my dad it hurts. Every time I stand in front of a mirror, it hurts. Old questions hurl back into my brain. Why did he leave? Would everything be different, or better, if he'd stuck it out with us? I swallow back tears as the elevator doors whoosh open at the lobby.

Outside, the incline takes me to the Chief Peguis Trail Bridge. Cars fly by and a bus whines down to a noisy halt at the stop. But there's no one walking. It's cold. There's too much snow.

I trudge over the bridge to Kildonan Park. I like the idea that I can disappear into the trees and brush of the bicycle trails or sit on a fallen trunk close to the river. There are plenty of corners of parkland on my side of the river, but I want to be away from my mom, my home, my friends — anybody who might ask questions.

The image of Mom on the edge, literally, on the edge of the balcony, swims in front of my eyes. What if I hadn't come home when I did? Would she have let go and fallen? It's too bizarre. I shiver. Maybe I should have been more sympathetic, but I was sure she was going to jump and that scared me.

What's the matter with her? Is it me? I try to think logically. The divorce? Maybe she's finally noticing that I've started wearing dark red lipstick and black eyeliner. Maybe it's the tight skirts and tops I bought with my Christmas money. Is she worried she's lost control of her darling daughter? That I'm becoming my own person? After all, I am almost fifteen! I've been waiting for her to flip out, but she hasn't mentioned any of those things yet, and she's not the type to disapprove quietly.

What if it's not what I'm doing? What if — now that I think about it, it's what she's stopped doing that's really weird. Apart from this afternoon, she doesn't talk like she used to. We hardly ever have actual conversations anymore. She rarely goes out with her friends. And she gave some ridiculous reason for not curling this year. What happened to her regular trips to the library, returning with a bag loaded with books?

She's not on my case about schoolwork like she used to be. She doesn't even ask about school! Mighty strange for a woman who insisted that homework be finished before I could even think about television or computer games and that all letters and numbers be neat and lined up just so. Does she know about my marks slipping? Is she ashamed of me, her once-upon-a-time straight-A kid? She hardly glanced at my last report card before signing it. But it's not that bad. Certainly not worth a jump off the balcony. It has to be the divorce. Or stress.

"Careful, Grandma Anne," says a voice. "It might be slippery."

Startled, I turn to see the tiniest old woman. She is hidden beneath a hat, hood and long coat. Her dark, empty eyes stare over a yellow scarf. She takes tentative steps while people, one on either side, hover anxiously.

"Hello." Her voice is deep and raspy. "Good to see you again."

"Come on now, Mother." The younger woman's smile is apologetic.

The person on the other side looks up, and my breath catches in my throat. It's Ryan Kostelniuk from my grade. He's new to my school. He's smart. He's gorgeous. Unfortunately, he's also oblivious to girls and painfully shy. When he realizes it's me, he stops.

"Hi," I say quietly.

"Hi, Sylvie." He doesn't meet my eyes.

"Sylvie!" Grandma Anne cries, her face animated. "Does this mean you and Ryan are dating again? I'm so pleased. He talks about you all the time."

"He does?" I gasp.

Ryan's already rosy cheeks flush scarlet. He tugs on her sleeve. "Let's keep moving. It's cold out here."

The younger woman, who I figure is Ryan's

mother, pats my arm. "Don't mind her."

Ryan struggles to get his grandmother to the other end of the bridge and away from his embarrassment. My mouth is still hanging open when he glances back.

I watch as they cross the road and get into a small white car. Grandma Anne thinks Ryan and I are dating. What a rush! But where would she get an idea like that? Has he really been talking about me? Maybe there was some other Sylvie at his old school. Maybe …

What a totally weird day!

Chapter Two

Mom is not home when I get back from the park. My stomach knots. I fly to the sliding doors. They are locked and freezing up again, but I open them, go onto the balcony and scan the parking lot. For what? Blood? The hideously mangled body of my mother? The chalk outline left by investigating police? Nothing.

Back in the apartment, I check the kettle. It has been emptied and returned to its place in the cupboard by the sink. Am I getting paranoid or what?

Then I see the note propped against the clock. "Dear Sylvie, Gone for a walk. Don't wait supper for me. Warm up some pizza. Love, Mom."

A walk. That's good. Walking relieves stress. And I don't mind pizza two days in a row. It sure beats Mom's gourmet cooking. Recently, very few dishes have turned out. I rummage in the fridge behind the plastic containers of singed couscous, overcooked fettuccine and soggy shrimp salad and find the pizza.

I zap two pieces of ham and pineapple in the microwave and pour a glass of milk. It's time to call Marissa.

"Hey, kiddo," she says. "And what exotic speciality are you chowing down tonight?"

"Leftover pizza."

"Homemade, no doubt."

"Nope. Bought. Delivered."

"You're kidding? Your mother actually ordered pizza?" She giggles. "Is she sick? I've known you guys since we were seven years old and you've never ordered in anything."

I sip my milk daintily while I listen — I hate when people slurp. Marissa definitely has a point about my mother.

"Oh well," she continues. "No doubt the napkins are folded and the table set perfectly."

I interrupt. "She drove Dad nuts when she started doing that. But she hasn't been so compulsively neat since he left." Which, I realize, was about the time my mother began acting strange. Even her regular cleaning binges became less frequent.

"She needs to get a life," says Marissa.

"Speaking of which, Mom almost threw hers away today," I say and launch into an account of the balcony scene and Mom's denial. I can almost taste my bitterness.

Marissa lets out a sympathetic whistle. "What did you do?"

I tell her about going to the park, about Ryan Kostelniuk and his Grandma Anne. Marissa shrieks with delight. "That's incredible! We'll have to give him the gears."

"No, we won't. We'll leave him alone. I think his grandmother is a bit crazy."

Grandma Anne's empty eyes haunt me.

"Poor Ryan," Marissa says. "Sounds like your mom is a little crazy, too." She makes an angry, snorting sound. "What is it with mothers these days? Mine's in bed, sleeping it off. Dad's home for a couple of days, though. She doesn't get so bad when he's around."

Another silence. Then, "How's your dad? Heard from him lately?"

The piece of pineapple in my mouth loses all flavor. "No."

"Sorry. He's probably just real busy."

"Whatever."

Marissa adored my dad. We used to have so much fun with him. Marissa was always included when we went skating or bowling or to restaurants. Then he walked out – two years ago. Marissa and I both lost.

Marissa's voice becomes brighter. "When do you think your mom might be going to the ballet again? Maybe I could come along, like before?"

"I don't know," I reply curtly. "We don't seem to do anything 'like before' anymore."

"Well, we're old enough to go by ourselves now. We'll go without her." She pauses. "I'd better go. Mommy dearest is yelling. Don't drip any pizza sauce on that nice clean floor. Bye."

I stare out the window, across the river, over the trees in Kildonan Park and on to the vast blue horizon. Good old Marissa. Always trying to cheer me up.

To take my mind off things, I plunk myself down on the piano bench and work my way through Hanon exercises, scales, triads and arpeggios. I get stuck on a tricky left-hand run in my sonatina and have to go over and over and over it. I get it if I go slowly. It's only because of the dome clock chiming six that I know how long I have been practicing. Three-quarters of an hour. Not nearly enough.

I work through two more pieces before the door knocker sounds. I open the door to find Mrs. Rathbone peering at me over her bifocals. Her white hair is gathered in a ruthless bun on top of her head, and she's wearing a pink and purple housedress and fuzzy slippers. She draws herself up, managing to come to my shoulder.

I can see beyond her into her apartment across the hall. The easy chair is covered with a yellow afghan. Cigarette smoke curls up from a ceramic ashtray on the arm — a fire waiting to happen. A commercial for adult diapers is playing on her TV.

To my surprise, she smiles. "I know we agreed that you'd stop practicing by six o'clock, but this isn't about your piano. Is your mother home?"

"No."

"Oh darn. I was hoping she was," cries Mrs. Rathbone. "I was hoping it wasn't her I saw out my window."

"What?" I squeak.

"Well, for the last while, every time I look out my window I can see this figure walking back and forth, up and down." She pauses. "You know my eyesight isn't so good, but I thought the person might be your mother — except why would your mother be walking back and forth, up and down?"

I dash into Mrs. Rathbone's smoke-filled living room and go straight to her window. Her apartment overlooks the sweeping front drive up to our block. A blonde woman wearing a white tracksuit is walking, with her arms folded, toward the front door. As I stand there, she turns and walks back up the street. She stops, pivots, looks around. What is she doing?

Mrs. Rathbone is behind me. "I hope you don't think I'm nosy. You don't, do you? I was wondering if this is some new exercise craze. Is it your mother, dear? She hasn't got a jacket on. She must be freezing."

I nod because I can't speak. The words are trapped in my throat. I mutter my thanks and leave. I grab my parka, one for Mom and the spare keys from the hook. The elevator is its usual slow self, but eventually I get to the main floor and out into the chilly evening.

Mom is poised where the sidewalk ends and the stairs to the new bridge begin. Her back is to me.

"Hi," I say, forcing a broad grin.

She spins around. "Huh?"

"I said, hi, how's it going," and I add, "Mom."

She squints. "Oh, it's you. I didn't see you."

"Tired of walking yet?" I ask, slipping her parka across her shoulders. "Are you cold?"

"You know, Sylvie, I am," she answers. "I was just thinking I should be getting back."

"Let's go in," I suggest. "It's past six-thirty. You must be starving."

"Yes, yes. Starving. What time is it?"

I gently push her ahead of me. That's twice today she's asked me the time — but she has in her green contact lenses and could easily have looked at her wristwatch. Besides, I just told her.

Before the elevator reaches our floor, she is completely herself. We acknowledge Mrs. Rathbone before she pulls her head back into her apartment.

The phone rings and Mom answers it. Her boots drop snow-covered gravel on the carpet. I follow on my hands and knees picking up as much of the mess as I can. I want her happy. Happiness might relieve stress.

"Hello. Marianne speaking," she says in her singsong manner. She pulls off her boots, and because I am right there, she smiles and hands them to me. She sits on the nearest chair while I put our boots neatly in the closet.

"Oh, it's you." There's only one person she would speak to in that guarded tone of voice. Valentino Marchione. My father. The man I have to see when it's mutually convenient, which is less and less often. After a few seconds she says, "Do you think it would be possible for you to come over? We need to talk. Wednesday's good. Thank you. Yes, Sylvie's here."

My jaw drops. Come over? She's always handed me over to him in the parking lot of the burger place at the end of the street. She gives me the receiver and heads for the bathroom, but not before I notice her tears.

I don't try to hide my surprise. "So, Dad, you're coming to see us."

"I reckon I am," he answers. "This is a first, her asking me over. But how are you, Sylvie? How is everything?"

I don't know what to say. I can't seem to get a clear picture in my mind, so I give him my mom's least favorite F-word. "Fine."

Chapter Three

After Dad's visit, I find myself in a corner booth in the burger place with the remains of a vanilla milkshake. The place is crowded. Marissa said she'd come if she could get away, but she's an hour late. Night has already turned the window into a mirror. While I wait, I stew about my parents' meeting.

Dad had said "Hi, Sylvie" and given me his usual charming but distant smile when he walked into our apartment. He had a soft look on his tanned face as he let his fingers drag along the back of the couch. Then his mouth hardened into a thin line when Mom entered and glared at him as though he was an intruder.

Her face was nothing compared to his stunned yet furious expression when Mom said, "What are you doing here?"

He looked at me. All I could do was shrug.

"You asked me to come, Marianne," he said in a cool tone. "What is it you wanted to talk about?"

Mom seemed flustered. "Pardon?"

Dad managed a wry smile. "I could ask you the same thing." Again, he turned to me. "What's going on?"

Mom crossed her arms. "Well, as long as you're here, you may as well sit down."

Dad perched uneasily on the arm of the couch. At first they talked about the weather, then about the weather in North Dakota. To be fair to Dad, he tried to keep the conversation flowing. Mom basically stared off into space, occasionally nodding and making some small comment. I did my bit. I even chatted about school and my junior-high graduation in June.

And then Mom leaped up from her seat and went to the front door. "Nice of you to drop by. Goodnight," she said. Dad raised his eyebrows but didn't argue.

I ran behind him as he marched to the elevator. "Don't mind her," I said. "She's under a lot of stress."

"I don't know what she's under," he replied, understandably annoyed. "I just wish she'd quit playing these stupid mind games. She's getting worse if you ask me. At least she didn't withdraw into herself like she does sometimes. That drives me crazy."

"Maybe you could've stayed longer — tried harder to find out why she wanted you to come over," I suggested. "It might've been important."

"She hates me. Pure and simple."

"She doesn't hate you," I argued. "You could've tried —"

The elevator arrived and he stepped in, cutting me off mid-sentence. "It was nice to see you, Sylvie. I'll call you."

"When?" I asked.

He smiled slightly.

As the doors whooshed shut, I yelled, "You should've tried harder! You give up too soon!"

But he was gone.

Mom was in the shower by the time I got back to the apartment. Lucky for her! I had a few choice questions for her, like what the heck did she think she was doing? She had invited Dad over. Why had she acted like he was some complete stranger who'd barged in?

I wrote Mom a note to let her know I was going out, then called Marissa and started to tell her what had happened, but she couldn't talk. Family crisis. She could probably meet me later at the restaurant. I'm still waiting.

"Mind if we sit?"

The black window mirror shows there are kids

standing at the table. I'm not in the mood for company other than Marissa's, and certainly not in the mood for these particular kids.

Before I can answer, Cassie motions for her group to slide in. Cassie – Snow Queen, untouchable, cool and beautiful, with her blonde hair, pale blue eyes and pale skin.

Jen sends me a stony glare. I'm in a stony mood myself and have no trouble returning the look, but in a way I feel sorry for Jen. She's colored her brown hair some sick blonde shade and pastes her face with white makeup base, but she still can't hide her red cheeks. She also can't hide the fact that she's nothing more than a Cassie wanna-be. Next comes Carleen – long red hair and green eyes. The guys drool over her, but they worship Cassie. Most girls would do anything to be a part of this group. I am not one of them.

Trent Thatcher drags a chair over and leans his elbows on the table. Orange hair sticks out from under his baseball cap. He winks at me and chomps on some fries. My cheeks burn. Trent has been the most popular boy forever – except that any kid with half a brain knows he's a jerk.

The only decent one is Royce Martin. What he's doing with these idiots, I don't know. He flashes me a bright smile and I smile back. Marissa would kill to be here. She thinks he's beautiful, with his dark skin and quiet ways. But she'd turn into a babbling idiot, she'd be so nervous. I, on the other hand, would kill to get out of this corner.

"Hey there, Sylvie," Royce says. "We just won our game."

Trent tips his chair back. "Royce here just wanted to hang with the leading goal scorer in the league. That's why he's here."

"Absolutely!" Royce slaps Trent on the shoulder.

Cassie raises her eyebrow at me. "Don't usually see you out alone."

"You look nice ... different," adds Jen.

"Thanks." I manage to stop my hands from running over the zippers of my new black vinyl jacket or from patting my slightly back-combed hair.

"Sylvie, do you want a burger?" asks Royce.

I shake my head and watch the people getting off the bus. No Marissa.

"Hey, we're talking to you!" cries Trent, reaching out and poking my arm.

"How'd you do on that science test?" Royce asks.

Trent doesn't give up. "Ryan Kostelniuk got ninety-seven. Did you beat him?" It's like a challenge.

I think about not answering, but then Trent would assume Ryan beat me and he'd tell everybody. I clear my throat.

"Ninety-eight."

Trent's laugh is victorious. "See, Cassie. I told you she was smarter than old cousin Ryan."

"Shut up!" snaps Cassie.

"He's your cousin?" My eyes widen with surprise.

Trent grins. "Yeah, second cousin. So my parents tell me I have to be nice to him."

Carleen tosses her red hair. "I still think Ryan's smarter."

I want out of here. Now! I push slightly against Cassie. "Excuse me. I'd like to go to the washroom. Could you please move?"

"Hey," says Cassie, "we just wanted to see if the queen of the study hall had been beaten by the new kid. Relax!" I'm shocked when she pats me gently on the wrist.

"Fine," I answer, refusing to go all mushy just because she sat beside me. "But I need to go to the washroom and then I have to get home."

She shrugs and slides out.

The next morning, Trent nudges me in the crowded school corridor. He winks and points to his hair, which is blue. He blows imaginary smoke from an imaginary gun and strolls off.

"Whoa," giggles Marissa. "What was that all about?"

"Oh, nothing."

She flips her long brown hair over her shoulder and leans into my face. "What do you mean 'nothing'? Something must've made Trent Thatcher crawl out from under his rock!"

I roll my eyes. "How would I know?"

She sneers after him. "And did you see his hair? Yesterday it was orange."

"And tomorrow it will probably be green." My eyes follow his bobbing blue head until it disappears. "And next week, fire-engine red. The week after that he'll be bald when his hair falls out from all the stripping and dyeing."

She laughs. I don't. We walk in silence, me in one of the short skirts and tight sweaters I've taken to wearing in the past few months. Marissa is in runners, blue jeans and a save the whales sweatshirt. As we reach the classroom, she turns to me.

"Do I detect a slight aura of depression here, or what? And you still haven't really explained the Trent thing. Time to 'fess up!"

"Oh, all right. He and Cassie sat with me last night when *you* didn't show up!"

Her eyes, so dark they don't seem to have pupils, nearly pop out of their sockets. "And you didn't call me? You didn't tell me?" She sighs as if controlling her temper. "Oh, never mind. So what happened?"

"Shhh," I whisper, "don't tell the *whole* world. It wasn't a big deal. I was waiting for you." I pause. "And Royce was there."

"No way!" she squeals.

My face grows warm when I realize why I haven't told her. I would have to leave out how good Trent's praise made me feel. I can't look at her. Instead, I stare at Ryan Kostelniuk as he makes his way down the hall. Our eyes meet, briefly.

Marissa nudges me, mischief all over her face. "So?"

"So nothing!"

I take a deep breath and follow a giggling Marissa into class. But when she sees my glum face she says, "Come on, old buddy. What's wrong?"

"Something's definitely not right with my mom," I say. "She's been changing somehow ... slowly."

"Examples," barks Marissa.

"It's hard to explain." I slide down in my chair and cross my arms. "It's been going on for a couple of years, but it's getting worse. It's like sometimes she doesn't see me, or doesn't know I'm there, or doesn't recognize me. She can't cook worth a darn. She loses things – keys, jacket, purse. But she hasn't really lost them. She just forgets where she's put them and then thinks they're lost or stolen. Meanwhile they're right where she left them. I think she's having some kind of eye trouble. She can't seem to tell the time. And the other day she went for a walk."

"So, what's wrong with a walk?" asks Marissa.

"She walked up and down outside our apartment block, over and over, and she didn't have a coat on, that's what's wrong! Then, she must not have closed the shower door last night because the floor was almost flooded this morning." I swallow hard, remembering. "The toothpaste lid wasn't put back on. The toilet wasn't flushed. The towels were all over the place."

Marissa peers deep into my eyes. "Our bathroom always looks like that."

"Well, ours doesn't!" My voice is getting loud and people are looking at us. "And she didn't do her exercises this morning and the radio wasn't on CBC." Tears gather in my eyes. "But you know what the real scary thing is, Marissa? She didn't even get out of bed this morning. I went to see if she was okay. There she was, in her clothes from yesterday! And she screamed at me to get out."

"Ahem, Sylvie," Marissa says in a gentle voice, "my mother is like that all the time."

"Yeah, but *your* mother is a drunk!"

She recoils as if I had slapped her.

"I'm sorry. I didn't mean it."

A voice booms from the front of the class. Mr. Gregory is waiting for everyone's attention.

"I'm really sorry." I try to touch Marissa's hand, but she pulls away. She ignores me as I stare at her, the tears running down my face. I'm a traitor. I collect my books and bolt for the door. I hear Marissa make an excuse for me. I lower my head and run down the hall.

Straight into the arms of Trent Thatcher.

Chapter Four

"Why, Sylvie, how nice."

I sidestep. Trent steps with me.

"Get out of my way," I whimper.

"Hey, what's up? You're crying?"

His blue eyes don't quite match his hair.

"Wanna talk or something?" he asks. "It's just phys. ed. next period. I was gonna skip anyway."

"You'll get into trouble," I say, conveniently forgetting the fact that I'm about to skip, too, for the first time ever.

"No problem," he says, gently heading me to the exit. "Don't start sounding like Ryan."

He helps me on with my jacket as we walk quickly out the side doors. I tuck my hands into my sleeves.

"You don't look like the type," he says out of left field.

"What type is that?"

"Oh, you know, the type to wear all those zippers, the ready-to-party type." He gives me a lopsided grin. Definitely cute. "How'd you get out of the house looking like this?"

"My mother wasn't paying attention. She hasn't been too worried about what I wear recently."

"Lucky you."

"Yeah, well, you can't judge a girl by her jacket." I wish I had worn my denim jacket with the fringes and the lamb's-wool lining or a good sensible parka.

"It's not just the jacket," he says. "There's the red lipstick." His eyes jump to my breasts and back up. "You're not geeky little Sylvie Marchione from kindergarten anymore."

"Geeky?" I glare at him. "I don't need this."

"Chill." He opens the door of the little restaurant. "I'll buy you a pop or something."

I stride ahead of him to the counter and order a milkshake. He orders an entire breakfast special. We sit upstairs by the window that looks down on Henderson Highway. I really want to talk – to tell him about my parents' divorce, my mother's weird behavior. But Trent rambles on about the hockey season, his computer, his bike, his childhood illnesses. He seems to forget he invited *me* to talk. So, I sip my milkshake and listen.

We return to school in time for lunch.

I hurry home after school. I have to pick up my music books and get to Mrs. Forrester's for my lesson. But I keep thinking about Marissa. What we'll say next time. *If* there is a next time. The look on her face. I'm such a bitch.

As I step off the elevator, my guilt is replaced by a gripping fear. Our apartment door is open — not wide, but open. Have we been robbed? Where is Mom?

I press my back against the wall just outside our apartment and slowly push the door open with my fingertips, like I'm a TV cop. The hinges squeak slightly.

My heart hammers against my rib cage. Do I go in? What if the robber is still inside? What if my mom is lying hurt somewhere? I take a deep breath and step in.

"Who's in here?" I shout. "Is anyone here?" Silence. "Mom?"

I tiptoe in, ready to run if anything's the least bit suspicious. The living room seems okay. I check my room. Neat as a pin. I squint into the bathroom. Messy — still!

I shove the door to my mom's room open with such force that it bangs against the wall. I see nothing unusual except that the sheets are off the bed and lying in a rumpled heap on the carpet.

"Sylvie, is that you, dear?" Mrs. Rathbone is walking into the living room, wringing her hands. "Oh, I'm glad you're home, dear," she says breathlessly.

"Why? What's happened? Why is the door open?"

She blinks with each of my questions.

"I don't know where to start." She gives an apologetic smile. "I don't want to appear nosy."

"Just tell me," I say curtly.

"About ten minutes ago, I started hearing a lot of banging coming from in here."

"Banging?" I repeat. "What kind of banging? What do you mean by banging?"

"Banging — like cupboard doors being slammed shut." She shakes her head. "And angry voices, well, one angry voice. Your mother's, dear."

I stare stupidly at her. "How could you hear all that?"

"I had my door open, of course," she says, taken aback. "But I wasn't spying, if that's what you're thinking, young lady. I was talking to a friend."

"Then what?"

"The next thing I know, your mother whips open your door." She demonstrates. "Just whips it open. And out she comes. Now, I don't mean to frighten you, dear, but she just didn't seem herself. A little wild eyed, I would say."

"Wild eyed?"

"That's right. She can't find any laundry soap, she says, and is going to the store to get some."

"What? Is she nuts? We just bought a humongous tub of laundry soap, two days ago, together." I walk to the little closet where we keep the cleaning stuff. I point to the yellow tub. "See? It's right here. No way she could've missed that."

"Maybe she didn't look in here."

"But this is where we always keep it."

"Well, I wouldn't know about that," Mrs. Rathbone says. "She was muttering something about the car. But I don't think she should drive, dear. She seems very upset. Maybe you can catch her in the parking garage. She can drive you to your lesson and get the soap."

"We don't need more — oh, right! Good idea."

I get my music case, usher Mrs. Rathbone out and fly to the elevator. It stops at the second and third floors on its way up.

I push "P" and hope for a speedy descent to the underground parking. No such luck. We stop on every floor. I am gnawing my lower lip by the time I get off.

"Please, please, let me see that green car. Please, please, be there."

I turn the corner. The car is right where it should be. Mom is frantically trying to get the key in the lock.

"What are you doing?" I sound as pissed off as I feel.

"Stay back," she says. Her voice is shaking. Her eyes do have a wild look.

"What do you mean 'stay back'?"

"Stay back," she repeats, thrusting her key ring into my hands. "Take them. Just don't hurt me."

Tears flood into my eyes. "What? I'm not going to mug you. Oh, Mom, what's the matter with you?" She stares vacantly. Frustrated, I stamp my foot like I used to when I was a little kid and not getting what I wanted. Right now, I want my mother to be herself. I want my mother to know who I am. "It's me. Sylvie. Your daughter! And I'm not old enough to drive. Why are you doing this?"

"Daughter? Sylvie! Of course." She laughs nervously and straightens her jacket. *My* jacket — the denim one with the fringes. It's as though she's only pretending to know who I am. I don't understand. She must be sick, very very sick. I have to get her upstairs. I have to get her to a doctor. Quick!

She tosses her head and says, "I couldn't see very

well. This place needs better lighting. I couldn't find the right key. I've fiddled with it so long that I've forgotten where I wanted to go."

She starts to sob, deep heartbreaking groans. I take her in my arms. She rests her head on my shoulder, which means she has to bend down a little.

"I'm so scared," she says. "I think I'm losing my mind, Sylvie. I'm so scared."

She's scared. I'm petrified.

I stroke her hair. Usually it is silky soft and tied with a fancy bow. Today it looks as though it hasn't seen a brush for a month.

"Shhh, shhh. It's all right. Let's go upstairs and I'll make us some tea."

"Okay," she says, like a three year old, sniffing and wiping her nose across the sleeve of my denim jacket.

She is composed by the time we reach our apartment. Mrs. Rathbone is hovering in the hallway.

"Oh, you caught up with her," she says, smiling broadly. "Now you can go to your piano lesson."

Mom turns to me, puzzled. "You have piano? Today?"

"It's Thursday, Mom."

"Well, then. You should get going." She nods toward the elevator.

"I'm going to call Mrs. Forrester and tell her

I'm not coming. You are not well."

"Don't be ridiculous. I'm fine."

"No, you're not!"

"Sylvie! Don't talk to me like that." That wild look has returned to her eyes.

Mrs. Rathbone pipes up. "Go to your lesson, Sylvie. I can stay with your mother until you get back."

"I'm not staying with you!" shouts Mom, her cheeks growing scarlet. "I don't know you."

Mrs. Rathbone clamps a pudgy hand over her mouth. I see understanding dawning in her eyes.

"Mom, Mrs. Rathbone is only trying to help."

"I don't want her in my house," Mom says, turning her back.

"But Marianne, dear," chimes Mrs. Rathbone in a stroke of genius, "surely you remember inviting me for coffee this afternoon. Oh, please don't tell me you've forgotten."

Mom brings herself to her full height. I wait for her to chew the old lady's head off. Instead, she gives us both a glowing smile. My mother has never invited Mrs. Rathbone or any other neighbor in for coffee – she guards her privacy – but she's so screwed up she'd rather take Mrs. Rathbone's word for it than appear rude and stupid.

"How silly of me," she says. "Do come in. And

don't mind the mess. I was changing the sheets on my bed."

"I know, dear," says Mrs. Rathbone. "Perhaps you'll allow me to help you with that while the coffee's brewing." She pushes my mom ahead of her and then whispers over to me, "Off you go, dear. I'll wait here."

"Are you sure?"

She smiles. "I'll be fine. We'll have coffee — even if I wasn't invited. Your mother won't know the difference."

Chapter Five

I sit on the polished black bench at the grand piano thinking about Mom handing me the keys to the car and how her fingers had been shaking. The pots of newly planted geraniums in Mrs. Forrester's living room send my thoughts skittering back to my mom on the edge of the balcony, "admiring the view," her fingers curled around the empty flower basket.

Now my own fingers are shaking and won't work. They slip and slide or hit two keys at once, causing Mrs. Forrester to make annoying little noises.

She's making one now. "Hmmm. Try again a bit slower and hands separately."

I'm doing a C major contrary-motion scale. I've been doing it for almost four piano grades without effort, but today my left thumb decides to cross under too soon and I run out of fingers.

"Hmmm. Let's try B flat major."

B flat major sounds wrong but I keep on with it,

then sit back with my hands clasped in my lap, my chin on my chest. I want to go home. I need to be at home. Be with my mom.

"Hmmm. How many flats are there in B flat major?" Mrs. Forrester asks. She's not really upset, just disappointed, concerned.

"Two."

"Did you play two flats, Sylvie?"

"I guess not."

"No, you didn't. I suggest you find some time for concentrated practice this week. These are easy scales. The scales you played earlier are for your exam, and they were even worse, weren't they?"

I nod and let my eyes wander. I love this room — its Royal Doulton china ladies in the cabinet, seascape oil paintings, silver candlesticks and blue carpets. It's like Mrs. Forrester, with her silver gray hair and blue eyes. Blue distracts me today. Trent's hair is blue. Trent is Ryan's cousin. Ryan has soft, shining eyes. He also has a Grandma Anne who thinks we're dating, who has empty eyes, who may be crazy. I think Mom is going crazy.

"What are you going to do about this?" Mrs. Forrester asks.

"Practice more. Concentrate."

"I can't play your exam for you." She opens my studies book.

I glance sideways to see if she's really mad at me. Her face is neutral. She has always been my piano teacher and I like her very much, but at the moment, she is bugging me because I haven't practiced enough and I've disappointed her. But mostly because I really don't want to be here.

"Perhaps you're just having a bad scale day." She grins. "When my music teacher would make a mistake, she used to say she had washed her hands and couldn't do a thing with them. Have you been doing too many dishes lately?"

I attempt a smile. "We have a dishwasher."

She places one long, elegant hand on my forearm. "Something is troubling you. Is it anything you want to talk about? I remember when your dad — "

"Not right now."

She nods and pats my arm. "All right then. We have two options. You can go home and I keep the money for doing nothing. This would put you one week behind in preparation for your exam. Or you can try to shut out whatever is bothering you and concentrate. You might feel better after doing your pieces."

"I'll try."

"Excellent."

I work my way through the music. She says nothing other than "Right," "Thank you," "Next one" or "Hmmm."

At the end of the painful lesson, she leads me to the door.

"Well, you'll be glad that's over," she says, not unkindly. "I sure am."

As I bend to tie my shoelaces, I have the urge to tell her to get lost and take the exam with her. I straighten up.

"Mrs. Forrester," I say, "I don't know if I'll be ready for my exam. I don't know if I'll be back."

"What?" Her shock gives me twinges of both conscience and pleasure. "You can't be serious, Sylvie. Musically speaking, your exam is around the corner. And it's paid for. I know you can do well. You've just had a couple of bad lessons. I'm sure you will be in fine form by – "

"I don't think so." I cast about for excuses. "I have a lot of homework. I won't have much time for piano."

"You've had homework before," she says, clasping her hands under her ample bosom. "Look, Sylvie. I can't make you come here. And I don't want you to come if you don't want to. But I want you to know that you are one of the finest pupils I have ever had the pleasure of teaching." She leans her crinkled, concerned brow down into my face. "You're not seriously thinking of quitting, are you?"

I swallow and don't move, in silent answer.

She draws back. Sadness settles on her face. "If you quit now, it will be a real shame."

I shrug and turn the ornate knob on the heavy wooden door. She covers my hand with hers.

"Give it another few months," she says softly. "Do the exam. Then if you want to quit, well, at least you'll have your grade six. Think about it."

"I have thought about it." That was partly true.

"Well, think more," she says, scowling. "Call me."

We lock eyes, blue against gray, until I look away. She lifts her hand and I turn the handle.

"I hope to see you next week, Sylvie. Take care."

I barely notice the bitter wind and stinging ice crystals on my face as I march home through the snow, or the blast of heat as I enter the apartment lobby. I'm almost afraid to go in.

My mother and Mrs. Rathbone are watching the news on TV. After hanging up my jacket and putting my shoes neatly in the closet, I drop my music case on the piano bench and perch on the arm of the couch.

Mom smiles. "Hey, Sylvie, how was your lesson?"

"Fine." She recognizes me!

"Ah, my least favorite F-word." She chuckles and her face suddenly beams with health and good humor. Her voice is relaxed and normal. Her hair is combed and held in place by two barrettes.

Mrs. Rathbone rocks back and forth a few times to heave herself out of her chair. She winks at me as she passes.

"We had a grand chat," she tells me. "We talked about the weather and how beautiful you are getting to be." I smile slightly at the compliment. "We did up the sheets and remade the bed."

I follow her out.

"You had one phone call, dear," she says. She creases her brow, obviously thinking hard. "Your father."

Mrs. Rathbone looks up at me, her expression one of deep distress. I move closer as she whispers, "I hope you don't mind, dear, but when she was in the bathroom, I took the liberty of phoning the doctor. I found the number in your mother's address book by the phone. I wrote the appointment on the calendar. I hope you'll forgive me, Sylvie. It was really an interfering thing to do."

"Then why did you do it?" I whisper back hoarsely, choked by her nerve.

"Because your mother needs help, dear."

"It's just stress," I say quickly. "Mr. Bartlet, her principal, told her to take some time off and see a doctor. She was probably going to make her own appointment pretty soon."

Mrs. Rathbone looks doubtful. "Is it possible for you to get time off school to go with her?"

I shoot a glance at my mom. She's channel surfing. "I'll check my timetable."

"Just be sure she keeps that appointment." Mrs. Rathbone wags her finger at me. "It might be nothing at all. But it might be something serious."

I start closing the door. "Thank you very much for all your help today."

"That's what neighbors and friends are for," she answers, unlocking her door. "I hope you forgive me for meddling."

She seems so small and frail. What can I say? "Of course."

"Be sure she goes," she fires across the hall.

Mom's voice makes me jump. She's right behind me. "Make sure I go where?"

"Oh, em, Mrs. Rathbone just wants to make sure you get to your doctor's appointment," I stammer, throwing home the dead bolt and fixing the chain. I punch in the security alarm – my birthday, 26 08.

"Why wouldn't I keep it?" She puts her hands on her hips and rolls her eyes. "She is a funny old girl."

I saunter into the kitchen. "What's for supper?"

She's right behind me again. "I don't know. What would you like? Maybe we could make something?"

"Maybe we could. How about some of your world-famous lasagna?"

"You're on."

I wrap my arms around her. Maybe coffee with Mrs. Rathbone brought Mom back to her old self.

She squeezes me in a bear hug and then scratches her head.

"Now, where did I put that hamburger meat?"

"The freezer."

"Well, of course." Mom laughs. "I was just kidding."

My delicate happiness is murdered. I don't believe her.

Chapter Six

When we're finished supper, I plod to my room and fall onto the pink and blue comforter. My room is pretty – white four-poster double bed and matching white furniture. All the cushions and chairs, even the curtains are in blues, purples and pinks, with some green. In front of the window there's an old armchair with a blue crocheted afghan over one of the arms.

I get a sudden urge to paint everything – midnight blue would be nice, or screaming scarlet, maybe rock-bottom black. Zigzags of orange or neon lime.

Marissa phones at eight o'clock and apologizes for making me cry and run out of class. I tell her it's not her fault and say good-bye quickly.

When Marissa phones back at eight-thirty, she says she's coming over, regardless. She says we have to talk – she needs me and I need her. I don't know whether I do or not. Mom has me all confused.

When Marissa arrives, Mom is taking a nap. Marissa plops into her usual place in the old armchair and says, "So, talk."

I stall. I'm mostly to blame for this morning's scene, and she's the one who's apologized. I should say I'm sorry, but the words stick in my throat.

And because I'm not talking, she does – rattling on about some new book she's reading and would I like to go to a movie on the weekend. She begins to tell me something about her mom and dad but I'm only half listening. Finally, I can't stand it anymore.

"Could you please just be quiet?" I sound really snarly.

She looks hurt. "Sure, if that's what you want."

"It's just that everything is so weird right now." I blow my nose even though I'm not crying. "I'm getting scared to death about Mom. I don't know what to do. I never know what she'll be like when I walk through the door. She didn't recognize me in the parking garage today."

"Maybe she was thinking about something else?"

"My own mother thought I was going to mug her and steal the car. I feel like I'm losing her. I've never been so scared in my whole life. Oh, Marissa," I cry, "what if she doesn't get better?"

"You could live with us," she says. We shake our

heads at the same time. "Nah, I suppose not." I could never be happy crammed into that little house with so many people. She finishes with "There's always your father."

"No way!" My fists clench at the thought. "He's always too busy. He doesn't have time for me. I'm gonna find out what's wrong with Mom so we can fix it. I'm taking her to the doctor next month, thanks to old Mrs. Rathbone."

"If there's anything I can — " Marissa starts.

"And my piano … what a crappy lesson! Mrs. Forrester knows something's wrong."

Marissa nods — she is listening. I pull another tissue from the box on my dresser. "When Dad left, I told Mrs. Forrester everything — how I begged him not to go and then how I begged Mom to let us go with him. I hated how angry they were. I hated how I felt inside … feel inside."

"I know," Marissa says.

I give her a wobbly smile. "I think I hurt Mrs. Forrester's feelings by not talking to her. I seem to be good at hurting people's feelings."

I stare out the window at the trees across the river. Marissa gives me time to say I'm sorry. I hear her sigh as she gives up hope.

"What happened to the nice, easy days — being a kid?" she says. "Swimming in the pool, tobogganing, skating at the park, pretending to be filthy rich and choosing what we'd buy from the catalog, sitting on your balcony watching the river."

"Gone," I answer in a small voice.

She smiles. "I miss talking to you. I mean, really talking and munching on junk food. I've been so busy looking after my brothers and sisters and – I'm kinda like you – I never know what shape my mom's gonna be in. That's why I didn't show up last night. You know, when you talked with Cassie and Trent and the airheads. I bet they liked your new clothes and fancy jacket. Why'd you buy that thing anyway?"

"Because I wanted to." I shrug, trying to look nonchalant. "I wanted something different."

"Must've cost a fortune," she says. "Did your mother have a bird?"

"No, she hasn't even ..." My voice trails off.

Marissa comes to stand beside me. "Hasn't even noticed? She really *is* losing it. The jacket's okay. But it's so ... so not you."

"Who says?"

She looks at me, hard, as if trying to see what's going on inside me. "And all this tight stuff you've been wearing?" She points at my outfit. "Is this you, too? We used to make fun of girls who look like that."

"Listen, Marissa," I say, barely controlling my

growing anger as my terrible day finally catches up with my emotions. "I'll wear what I want, when I want."

She folds her arms. "Just trying to find out what's going on in my best friend's life."

I fold my arms right back at her. "I thought friends weren't supposed to care about what you wore. I thought friends were friends no matter what."

Her eyes narrow. "Why are you so pissed off at me? I haven't done anything. *I'm* the one who should be mad. At you. Keeping things from me. Insulting my mother in public."

"Huh!" I spit out the words. "*That* was just the truth."

A veil falls over her eyes. "I think I should go now before we both say stuff we might regret."

"Good idea." My tone is perfectly even and perfectly cold as I open the bedroom door. "You may recall that I didn't invite you over tonight."

She pauses just outside my room. "You say your mom has changed. You've changed, too." Pity is written all over her face.

My blood begins to boil. "Maybe I haven't changed," I hiss. "Maybe this is the real me finally coming to the surface. What do you think of that?"

She doesn't argue or get mad – doesn't say anything. Just slips into her beat-up coat and boots and goes out.

Chapter Seven

Dr. Gina Caswell's office is on the seventh floor of the Medical Arts Building. I sit staring out the window at the heavy clouds.

I think of how distant Marissa and I have become. Then I think of Trent. Once or twice in the past month he's swaggered into the library and sat at my table. His roots are showing below the blue spikes of hair. I think about Ryan. He doesn't so much as glance in my direction when I see him in the library. But if he ever did, I'd like to talk about his Grandma Anne.

I look at my watch. Mom has been in with the doctor for almost half an hour. And we waited half an hour before that. My right leg jumps and wiggles, a sure sign of my impatience.

The man across the small room is frowning at me. I don't know if it is because of my clothes or my dark lipstick or my restless leg. I get up and rifle through the old magazines in the rack by the door. I choose one and sit down.

Dr. Gina comes out and signals to me. I go with her into one of the examination rooms. She's about the same age as Mom. Her dark hair is in a tight perm, but her white coat hangs loosely on her tall frame.

"Sylvie, I wonder if I might ask you a few questions."

It's a statement, not a question. I nod.

"Your mother's getting dressed, so we only have a few minutes." She drums on the counter with her fingernails. "I'm a bit concerned. Are you?"

I shift in my chair. "That's the understatement of the year."

"Has she been exhibiting any strange behavior? Acting out? Getting lost? Forgetting things?" she asks, still clicking her nails against the desk.

"It's just stress." I shrug.

"I'm not so sure, Sylvie. Please answer my questions."

My heart sinks. "All those things."

"Can you give me any examples? Anything out of the ordinary?"

I look at her worried face. I guess if there is anywhere I should talk about the balcony and the kettle, it's here, with this lady who has been my mother's doctor for years. But what if I give incriminating evidence and make things worse for my mother?

Dr. Gina sighs. "I know this is hard, Sylvie, but nobody knows her better than you do. I need your help. She needs your help."

"Okay, okay," I say, picking at a nonexistent thread in my skirt. "One day I came home from school and she was out on the balcony. She was on a stepladder, but she had one foot on the railing. She had this really weird look on her face, like she was going to jump. We live on the tenth floor." I stop. I can't meet Dr. Gina's eyes, so I blink at the chart on the wall behind her.

"What did you do?"

"I tried to get her to come down, but I don't think she heard me."

"How did you get her down?"

"I didn't. The phone rang. She turned around, did this quick little jump and answered the phone like nothing was wrong."

"Did you question her about it?"

"She said she was fixing the hanging basket and admiring the view."

"How did she seem afterward?"

"Like normal."

"Really?" Dr. Gina's pen is flying across the yellow lined paper.

"Okay, so not normal. We had a fight over the fact that she put the electric kettle on the stove to boil."

"Has she been losing her temper a lot lately?"

"More than a lot."

"How long would you estimate she has been acting strangely?"

"A couple of years, maybe. But lately, she's been getting worse. Really bizarre. She's been going out for walks – without a coat, without boots."

"I understand that it was the principal from her school who suggested she come see me, is that right? Do you know what happened there?"

"Not really. You'll have to ask her."

"I did. She doesn't know why, except that the principal says she can't control her classes. There seems to be quite a lot she doesn't know." Dr. Gina's chair squeals as it swivels. "Does your father know?"

"I guess so. I don't know."

"Your mother wants you to have a family meeting."

"She does?" I frown. "What does she want to talk about?"

"Ask your father to call me," Dr. Gina says, rising. "Right now, we'll get your mother some tests. That way we can discover if there is an organic cause for her behavior."

"Organic?" I leap to my feet. "Like a disease? Isn't it just stress?"

"I don't think so, Sylvie."

"Depression?"

"Maybe, but – "

"But what?" I'm trying not to panic.

"Let me get the lab results, okay?" She opens the door. "We don't want to jump to any conclusions."

"Is there anything I should be doing – like right now?" I want to grab her by the lapels and shake her until I get an answer, a cure, pills. Something.

She ushers me out. "I'd like you to keep a record for me. You know, if you notice anything different, or if she gets worse, that sort of thing. And, please, call me anytime, particularly if you think she is going to hurt herself." She pauses. "Or you. Probably your father should be more involved. Take care, Sylvie. I'll see you soon."

That's it. Class dismissed. Just drop a few bombs and walk away. Get my father involved? I don't think so. He's too busy to be involved with me, never mind Mom. After their last disastrous meeting, I doubt he wants to be in the same room with her.

I follow Dr. Gina into the waiting room, where she calls in the frowning man. Mom is waiting by the desk, clutching a fistful of lab requisitions and talking to the receptionist. Mom's top two buttons are done up wrong.

I rush to her, laughing lightly.

"Oh, Mom, can't take you anywhere." I fix the blouse.

"How embarrassing," she says, growing pink. "I didn't notice."

"You're worse than a little kid." We both should get Oscars.

We make a quick exit. Mom pushes the button for the elevator and leans against the wall.

"Dr. Gina asked me so many questions," she says. "And I had to draw this stupid square and triangle thing. You know how bad I am at drawing."

I laugh. "Yeah, you can't even draw stick people."

She shakes her head. "I didn't do a very good job on the square. Dr. Gina was surprised, even though she tried to hide it. And then I had to count backward from a hundred by sevens. Who can do that? Can you?"

"100, 93, 86, 79, 72, 65, 58."

"I couldn't get past 93." Her eyes are flooding with tears, but she keeps smiling. "Have you ever tried to recite the months of the year backward?"

I close my eyes. "December, November, October, September, August."

"August comes before September, doesn't it?"

"Yeah, if you're saying them forward."

"Damn!"

She rubs her forehead and looks so sad that I reach out and touch her arm. "I'm sorry, Mom."

"I'm sorry, too," she whispers. "Something is happening to me. Every now and then it's like a light goes on and I am ... me. The next time the light goes on, I'm in a completely different place. People talk to me like they are my best friends and I haven't a clue who they are."

The elevator lets us out and we enter the lab. I hold her purse and coat while she gives blood and urine samples and has a chest X-ray. Finally, she emerges, pale and limp and complaining of a dreadful headache.

All the way home on the bus, she keeps her eyes shut and her head resting on the window. She won't talk to me. We stop in the lobby to get the mail. She does a quick once-over of the letter and bills while we enter our apartment and then drops the pile of envelopes onto the kitchen table.

"You read them," Mom says. She tosses her coat across a wingback and kicks off her shoes.

"But you always read the mail. I thought it's one of the things you look forward to. You read it. I'll make us some soup for lunch. I gotta get to school."

She glares at me and goes into the bathroom. I follow her and watch as she reaches into the medicine cabinet for the extra-strength painkillers —

the ones with codeine that she has left over from a sinus infection. She wrestles with the bottle, trying to get the cap off. Frustrated she thrusts it at me.

"You do it." And then, almost as an afterthought, "Please."

One quick twist and strong flip of the childproof lid and it's open. She grabs the bottle, shakes out two pills and crunches them with her teeth.

"Yuck!" I screw up my face. "Aren't you going to drink some water with those?"

"Good idea," she says, as if I'd come up with some new concept, and fills the blue glass with water. I watch as she swallows. She gives me the half-empty bottle to cap, which I do with a loud snap.

"Mom, there seems to be a lot of mail. Didn't you get it yesterday?"

She gives me a stupid grin. "Dunno." She pushes past me. "Look, Sylvie, I'm not hungry. I'm going to bed to get rid of this headache."

I follow her to her bedroom. "You should eat. Maybe some food will …"

Mom's room looks like a hurricane has torn through. The duvet is on the floor, the sheets in a heap beside a pile of other clothes. The oak dresser is littered with underwear and bits of white paper. Several books, all open, look as though they have been swept aside and left where they fell.

"Oh, don't worry about me," Mom says, gathering the duvet and crawling onto her bed. "You have your lunch and go to school. I'll see you when you get home."

I back out and close the door quietly. Something is very, very wrong.

I decide not to make soup, so I won't have to tidy up. Instead, I reach for some crackers, a cheese slice and a cola, which I gulp down while staring out the sliding door. In the breeze, the hanging basket sways on its loose hanger, sending a shiver down my spine.

I stick my arms into my vinyl jacket and my feet into my granny boots, although I know I should wear my parka and felt-lined boots because it's snowing. I set the alarm and leave. But as the door clicks behind me, I panic — what if something happens to Mom?

Across the hall, Mrs. Rathbone's door is slightly ajar. I knock. "Mrs. Rathbone? Can I speak to you please? Mrs. Rathbone?"

She sticks her head out. "Oh, hello, dear. Everything all right?"

"I only have a few seconds," I say, quickly fumbling in my back-pack for a piece of paper and a pen. I scribble down the alarm code. "Here's the key and this is our security number. Mom is in her bedroom sleeping."

"Did you go to the doctor?"

"Yes, and now she has a headache."

"The doctor has a headache?"

"No, my mom."

"I know that, dear. I was making a little joke." She chuckles behind her hand.

"I gotta go."

"Okay, dear," she calls as I take off down the hall at a jog. "I'll keep my door open a bit so I can hear if there are any noises."

Chapter Eight

I'm late. I take the seat beside Marissa, but she doodles in her notebook and ignores me. Not surprising.

"Glad you could join us, Sylvie," says Mr. Sisson. Marissa and I think he's so handsome. His brown eyes sparkle beneath his heavy eyebrows as he peers at me.

I give a sheepish grin. Mr. Sisson nods and a strand of hair falls forward. From habit, I glance at Marissa for her reaction — some habits are hard to break. But she looks away without her usual smile.

When the buzzer goes, I start after Marissa. I want to tell her about Mom, but Mr. Sisson steps in front of me and I almost run into his gray shirt.

"Sit down, Sylvie," he orders. I sit. "I've been hearing some strange things about you. Running out of a class. Skipping — you missed an essay outline, by the way."

"I had to take my mother to a doctor's appointment."

"Really?" His tone annoys me. He thinks I'm lying. "If she's that ill she should've been taken by ambulance. Or maybe she's forgotten how to drive."

How dare he talk to me like this? I have high marks ... well, up until the last few months. I refuse to acknowledge the tiny voice inside reminding me that I didn't have a note for missing the morning, and I haven't done a stitch of homework in three days. Besides he's right. Mom *is* that ill and she *has* forgotten how to drive. She can't even unlock the car door.

"I'm telling the truth. We took the bus."

"Sure. Listen, here's some more truth. I've noticed a big difference in you since Christmas. Your grades are dropping, not a lot, but enough." He smiles slightly. "You're such a fine student. I don't want you to blow it. I want to nip this thing in the bud. Understand?" he says, straightening his tie.

"Yes, sir." I hope my voice remains neutral.

"I've been teaching long enough to know the signs of a student in trouble. You're a good kid. Hang in there."

Marissa is lounging just outside. I want to throw my arms around her and sob with relief, but I can't move.

"Boy, Sisson figures you're turning into the next high-school dropout by the sound of it." She clicks her tongue. "Your marks must really be getting bad — way down in the nineties instead of hundreds?"

I don't need her sarcasm but I don't want to get into another argument. "In the subjects I don't like. I just don't see the point."

"I sweat my brains out and get seventy-five," Marissa says. "You don't bother to study, or you forget, and still ace tests. You're lucky, you know. You shouldn't blow it." She flips her long hair over her shoulder. "So, I just want to tell you I know what it's like to be so messed up in your head that you can't think straight. I just wanted to tell you that. Anyway, I've got grocery shopping to do tonight and tons of other stuff."

She seems uncomfortable — like she's trying to patch things up before leaving town or something.

I want to keep her with me, want to say more but don't know what. "I want to tell you about ..." I call out but she hurries away. I get my books and head for my next class, a cold loneliness settling in my heart.

"Hey, Sylvie."

Trent pushes through the crowd and holds out his arms wide.

"I'm taking a poll. What do you think?"

I'm speechless. His hair is buzzed short — and it's brown! His grin fades as he waits for my answer.

"Nice."

A huge grin splits his face as he backs down the stairs.

He points his imaginary gun at me and fires.

Chapter Nine

Marissa and I have managed to avoid each other for the past two weeks. We've taken to sitting on opposite sides of the classroom, and I've noticed she's missed more school than usual. Today, she sneaks out early while Mrs. Kovacs, the math teacher, shakes her fist at her remaining students, the loose skin of her upper arm wagging.

"And make sure you have the answers to these equations on my desk by Wednesday," she rasps. "Or else or I'll track you down and cause you grievous bodily harm. Remember, I know where you live. This is my last year teaching, and I don't want any of you flunking my class."

Some kids groan, some laugh. She's timed her threat for right before the buzzer goes, to end our Friday with a bang.

I stare at her as she moves slowly in front of the neatly written math on the blackboard. I wonder if

I really can get this assignment done, with all the other homework I've put off. She fires me a bright, cheerful smile as I leave the classroom.

Marissa's coat and many of her books are gone from our locker by the time I get there. Just as well. What would I say? Except that perhaps we are both being over-sensitive. I know that she always likes to beat the Friday night mob at the grocery store and so I know, in my heart, that this time, she's not intentionally avoiding me. It just feels that way.

I stuff texts and notebooks into my back-pack and carry those that won't fit. I feel like a mule as I make my way across the student parking lot. Trent and Ryan are leaning against the wall. Cassie is batting her eyelashes at Ryan.

Trent waves, positively beaming, but it's Ryan's slow smile that gets me.

"Hi, Sylvie," Trent says.

I nod and mutter hello to him and Cassie. Then I give Ryan a direct stare and say, "How's it going?"

"Okay," he replies, turning bright pink. "How's it going with you?"

"Okay."

"That's good. Well, I'd better get home. Bye."

So much for my brilliant conversational ability. Darn! I watch him walk away. He has a powerful stride, as though he's ready to take on the world.

Cassie sighs. "I don't get it. What's with that guy? He's so … I dunno … so hard to reach. Look at him walking like he owes nothing to nobody."

"Who knows what's up his nose," Trent mutters. "He's starting to bug me, big time."

"Whatcha doin' this weekend?" Cassie asks me.

I blurt out an answer. "I've got tons of homework."

"We're having a party tonight," she says. "Wanna come?"

"I don't know."

Trent takes a deep breath. "It's at my house. My parents are going to a wedding in Calgary for the weekend. I can't go, because, gosh darn, someone has to stay home to feed the dog. That somebody would be me and Ryan. They figure Ryan will keep the place in one piece."

"Everybody's coming over around nine." Cassie looks down her nose at me even though I'm taller.

"So late?" I ask, immediately feeling like a jerk. "It's just that, well, my mom doesn't like me out too late. I'm usually home by eleven."

"Come on." Trent gives me one of his adorable grins. "It'll be fun."

"I'll have to check the bus times."

My heart is jumping around. Marissa and I have wondered about these parties. I shouldn't go without her, but Friday nights her mother goes out, and

Marissa has to stay home to take care of her brothers and sisters after shopping.

"I'll call you later," I tell them. "It all depends on how my mom is feeling."

"Whatever!" answers Cassie. "And don't bring that nerdy friend of yours. What's her name? Oh yeah, Marissa."

I figure she thinks it's safe to invite me because I won't show without Marissa.

It is only due to years of practice that I make it all the way home without losing control of the heavy books clutched to my chest. I manage to unlock the lobby door, press the elevator buttons and get into our apartment.

Then I drop everything.

Chapter Ten

Photograph albums lie scattered, plastic pages torn, recklessly tossed along the hallway and into the living room. Mom is sitting, cross-legged in the middle of it all, with each and every photograph in her lap, around her feet or pressed to her chest. When she looks up, it's clear she's been crying. She is still wearing the clothes she went to the doctor's office in and then slept in.

"Hi, Mom," I say in a low voice as I remove my shoes and vinyl jacket. No answer. I skirt around the album labeled "Sylvie: Elementary School" and dump my books on the desk in my bedroom.

How could she! Those albums contain my life, not just hers. But she seems so pathetic and so sad that my temper settles down. I sigh and lean against the bedroom door to close it.

The sound of my mother's sobs breaks through. I wonder if I can be trusted not to strangle her. I change into jeans and a red T-shirt and take several deep breaths before leaving my room.

I sit beside Mom and put my arm around her shaking shoulders.

"What's wrong?" I ask softly. "Why did you take all the photos out of the albums?"

"It must've taken a long time."

I'm not sure what she's talking about, so I guess.

"You mean to get the photos all arranged? Not really. We did it bit by bit — "

She waves her hand in my face. "No, daughter, it must've taken a long time for me to get like this."

Daughter?

"Crazy," she says, wiping her nose on the back of her hand. "A long time to get crazy."

"You're not crazy, Mom." I give her a little hug. "You're just stressed."

"This is not stress." She takes in the scattered memories on the floor with a swoop of her arm. "This is insanity. I took them all out."

"Why *did* you take them all out?" I look down on a wedding picture of her and Dad taken on the footbridge in Kildonan Park. Apart from a few fine wrinkles around her eyes, she doesn't look much different, although Dad's black hair is streaked with gray now.

And there's the photo of Dad and me building a

sandcastle at Grand Beach. Another of us horseback riding. One of me at five years old, dressed as a dragon for Halloween, holding Dad's hand. Mom and Dad at the hospital with a newborn baby, me, in Dad's arms.

Mom blinks at me. "I don't know anybody in these pictures. Why do I have pictures of strangers? It makes me very sad and very lonely. I recognize myself in some – and you. Who are these other people?"

She looks so blank I figure it would be useless to start telling her who everybody is. I get her to the couch and hand her a tissue and the remote control. Immediately, she starts surfing.

This can't be happening. As I choke back my tears, I gather the memories into heaps, close the albums and put them back in the bookcase drawers. One day, when I have time, I'll sort them all out.

"It must've taken a long time," she says again. "A long time."

Did it take a long time? Or was it sudden?

I mentally check off all the weird happenings – the balcony, the kettle, the walking back and forth, the bathroom, her bedroom, the laundry soap, her arguing, the car keys, the mail, her mind games with Dad and now this. She seems to know she's not well, but the "why" slips away as she reaches for it.

The dome clock chimes five. I should practice my piano, but what for? Yesterday, on the phone, I told Mrs. Forrester I wouldn't be coming back. Again. But I *could* do twenty minutes, or scales, or just the sonatina – but I'm not in the mood.

"A long time." Mom shakes her head.

"I'm going to make supper."

She jumps up. "I'll help, daughter."

"I'm only warming up leftovers." I can't help being annoyed at how she is right beside me, yet can't remember my name.

"That's great." A smile brightens her red-rimmed eyes. "Anything I can do?"

"The microwave will do all the work," I retort, unable to control my sarcasm.

Her brightness fades and she returns to the couch with her shoulders slumped. I put two portions on plates and into the microwave. While they are heating, I pour two glasses of milk, set the table, not forgetting napkins – which were a must for my once etiquette-conscious mother – and plug the kettle in for tea. When the microwave bell dings, I call Mom to the table. I have to remind her to wash her hands, and she does so like an obedient child. I join her at the table after making a pot of tea.

Dinner is silent, so different from when we'd tell each other about how the day went. I think of

Marissa as I push a microwave-hardened piece of pasta around. Marissa is always going on about how well Mom and I communicate and how lucky I am.

"Mom, you know Trent Thatcher?"

No answer.

I keep trying. "He has this cousin ..."

Her eyes are empty — like I'm not here. I puff out my cheeks and blow out a stream of exasperated air. What's the point?

I push my plate away. Mom is stuffing her face. When she looks hungrily at my half-eaten food, I give it to her, and she inhales that too. Tomato sauce rings her mouth. The napkin remains untouched.

Dr. Gina's request for a list suddenly seems like a good idea, and I excuse myself to start one. I include everything I can think of — and when they happened — so I can compare them to ... whatever might come next.

I half shut the bedroom door and decide to start with math before Mrs. Kovacs causes me grievous bodily harm. The numbers and signs swim in front of my eyes, I give up and start in on the novel I have to read, but it's such a depressing story that I toss it aside. I do better with my grammar and finish most of the assignment.

The digital clock reads seven-thirty. I go get a drink.

The table is not cleared. Tomato sauce and bits of cheese are stuck to the plates and forks. Milk is forming stubborn circles on the bottoms of the glasses. Mom's cup is clean. The teapot is still full. Mom is channel surfing. I don't say anything but make a lot of noise to let her know she could at least help clean up. I can't stand that blank stare. The silence is terrible. And she says *she* feels lonely!

Marissa must be home by now. I decide to quit being stupid about our relationship and phone her.

"I'm busy," she says as soon as she finds out it's me. "I've got to —"

"I hate this!" I interrupt and go through the whole supper thing.

"Talk to your dad." Marissa sounds as though she's softening slightly. "This is a family problem, Sylvie, not just your problem."

My voice is tight and squeaky. "I don't want another family problem."

"Don't cry!" she says with some of her usual sympathy. "But this obviously isn't something you can deal with on your own anymore. And I can't help you!"

I sniff. "Remember when we were little — when Mom let us help her make cookies, weed the flower garden. She'd take us out for supper once a month — or more when Dad was really busy working. And every Christmas going to the ballet. Remember all those trips to the library? We'd come home with *so* many books. She never goes anywhere now."

"Sylvie, I've gotta go!"

"Even though she's sick or stressed, whatever, I figured —"

Marissa shouts at someone at her house. "I'm coming!" Then to me she says, "I can't talk now, even though *you've* suddenly found the time."

"I mean, I've heard of old people getting senile and losing their minds, and Mom *was* thirty when she had me, but she's not *that* old."

"Sylvie, please, I —"

"My own mother has forgotten my name! Does that mean she doesn't want to remember? That she doesn't really want me around?"

"Look, Sylvie. I've gotta hang up now. Bye!"

Chapter Eleven

The door knocker rat-a-tat-tats. A brief glance around the kitchen and living room to make sure everything is tidy and then I swing open the door.

"Hi, Sylvie. Are you ready?" says Dad, hugging me. "How come I had to meet you here instead of down the road? I'm not real comfortable with this — after last time."

"How's work?" I ask, indicating for him to sit down.

He peers down the hallway. "Where's your mother?"

"Oh, she's in her room." I try to smile but my lips are getting ready to quiver.

He raises his eyebrows and looks like he wants to ask a million questions. He perches on the edge of the couch. Marissa's right. I need his help.

"How's work?" I ask again.

"Work's work," he replies. His standard answer.

"Keeping busy. I'm lining up job crews for summer. Some new buildings happening on the outskirts of town." He leans forward. "But I'd rather talk about you — about us — you and me. I don't like how things are. I don't see you enough. But I don't think this is the place to talk about —"

"I don't want to get into that," I say. Surprise registers on his face. "Mom's in her bedroom. I want to talk to you quickly, before she realizes you're here. I think Mom is sick."

"Sick? How?"

"Shhh. I don't want her to hear."

"I think you'd better start at the beginning."

I take a deep breath. "I don't know when the beginning is, but that day you called and she asked you to come here, Mr. Bartlet, the principal, sent her home from school and told her to go see a doctor."

"And?"

"And when I got home from school that day, I ..." What do I tell him? *How* do I tell him? "I found her at the edge of the balcony. I was sure — still am sure — she was thinking about jumping off. Then we had this big fight about the kettle. She thought it was the kind that you boil on the element instead of an electric one. She would've melted the thing if I hadn't stopped her. And there's more — Mom has had a bunch of blood tests but she has to have a CT scan and a puncture or something."

"Sylvie," he says softly, touching my hand. "What are they testing for? Do you know?"

I pull my hand away and shake my head. "I just want you to see if you notice anything wrong while you're here."

He leaps to his feet and starts for Mom's bedroom. "It's time for me to talk to her — sick or not. I need to get some things straight."

"Wait. You don't understand ..." I whisper hoarsely.

He glares at me for what feels like a long time. "Is that so?" Then he knocks. "Marianne, it's me, Valli."

"Who?"

"Valli. Valentino."

"Who?"

Dad glances at me, confusion growing in those familiar gray eyes. "It's me, Valentino, Valli, your husband."

"Ex-husband," I remind him.

"Go away!" Mom shouts.

He shouts back. "Stop fooling around, Marianne! Come out and talk to me or I'll come in."

"Go away. I'm not ready to see you."

"What do you mean, not ready to see me?

What's to get ready?" He barges in.

The room is the same mess I had seen earlier. But it isn't the room that has Dad stopping dead in his tracks, it's Mom. I gasp in disbelief.

Her blonde hair is piled high and clasped at the side by a diamanté clip. Diamond drop earrings sparkle just above the single strand of glowing diamonds at her throat. Her dress is a shimmering creation of azure.

"Going somewhere?" I ask, finally getting past my shock.

"Just trying it on," she says. "I was thinking how long it's been since I went out anywhere special."

"You look fantastic," Dad says.

A bright smile flashes across her face. The childish pleasure in her eyes rips at my guts.

"So, why don't you take me to dinner?" she asks him.

Dad's jaw falls. "I'm not exactly dressed for it, but if you'd like we could go to that new restaurant downtown."

"Terrific," she answers, slipping past us into the hallway.

"But Mom," I say, grabbing her arm, "you just ate. Remember?" She gently dislodges my fingers and smiles like I'm some silly little kid.

"I thought you said she was sick," Dad mouths at

me behind her back, and then in a normal voice says, "What about you, Sylvie? Wanna join us? It's been a long time."

I wouldn't mind doing the family thing but I'd rather go to Trent's. "I think I might go to Marissa's for a while, if that's okay."

Why don't I just tell them the truth? Maybe I'm afraid they won't let me go to Trent's because his folks are out of town. Maybe it's just easier to lie.

Dad takes a coat for Mom from the closet – he still looks stunned by her glamour – opens the door and steps into the hall. Mom comes over and pecks me on the cheek. She's overdone the perfume.

"Be good," she says. "You really don't mind if I go out with him, do you?"

"Since when do I have any say in what you do?"

She grins. "I'll show those doctors there's nothing wrong with me. Bye, daughter."

I don't know whether to laugh or cry. I flop onto Mom's messy bed. Something sharp pokes me in the back. It's a hanger and on it is the price tag.

A thousand dollars! No wonder she didn't say anything when I bought my vinyl jacket.

I pull Dr. Gina's list from my pocket and add the dress and dinner with Dad. Maybe Dr. Gina will have some answers next time.

An uncomfortable sadness seeps into my bones.

My mom is slipping away from me in some unnatural, painful way. She is somehow trapping me and shutting me out at the same time, and there is no help for either of us.

I reach for the phone.

Chapter Twelve

An hour later, I press Trent's doorbell. He lets out an appreciative whistle when the wind blows my unbuttoned jacket open.

"Look at you! And those legs! Wow!"

I manage a hello and head for the bathroom to brush my hair and touch up my lipstick. I smooth out my short black dress, check that the skinny ties at the shoulders are tight over my white T-shirt and adjust the bolero-style sweater. I can only hope that my makeup doesn't look stupid. And that, unlike Mom, I don't have on too much perfume.

Trent's small house is pulsating with the thump-thump-thump of bass speakers. He ushers me in through the kitchen, where pop bottles and potato chips litter the counters and table. He pushes me into a living room the size of my bedroom — it's packed. Every piece of furniture holds a person. The wood and glass coffee table has three girls propped on it. My mother would freak. Kids sit in corners, on cushions all over the floor or against the doorframe. Some are lounging against the walls, deep in conversation. I know most of them from school or the community center. Everyone has a drink of some kind. Two girls are smoking over by the open window. I can hear them talking – about graduation, which is coming up in two months.

Ryan nods at me from the floor. He's sitting in the dimmest corner.

Carleen glances over at me from her perch on the arm of the couch. She's in jeans and a green ribbed top. Her red hair is caught back in a velvet headband. Jen, totally cool in a short yellow dress, is flipping through some CDs and doesn't look up.

Cassie waltzes over – "So you made it. You never cease to amaze me." – and waltzes back to her throne, an extremely comfortable-looking chair. Her blue silk top hangs almost to her knees, black tights hug her legs. I feel ridiculous. I don't fit in here – all these beautiful, popular people. I'd rather be warm and relaxed with Marissa.

Trent hands me a plastic glass. "Here. Hope you like it."

I take a sip and find it very pleasant, so I take a gulp.

"Turn down the music!" Trent screams. "I can't

make polite conversation. Turn it down."

"Hey, Sylvie," calls Royce. "I figured you'd bring Marissa."

"She couldn't come." I do believe he looks disappointed. She'd be over the moon, but I refuse to think about what she's going to say when and if I tell her I went to this party without her.

The boys get talking, and I fade into the general noise of the room. I meander over to the different groups of girls and have fairly decent conversations. Time goes by quickly and pleasantly enough until Trent starts to tell a joke about a priest, a rabbi and a minister having dinner in a restaurant. All at once I get the ridiculous image of Mom in her expensive dress in a classy restaurant with her ex-husband, doing ... saying ... who knows what. It's weird. I start to laugh, not a giggle, but a real stomach-splitting bellow. I think I'm hysterical.

"What's so funny?" asks Carleen. "Has he got to the punch line?"

I can't answer, so I head for the kitchen. The first thing I see is a blue tea kettle on the back element of the stove. I bury my hands in my hair.

"Hey, what's this?" Cassie strolls in with Carleen.

"Mom tried to boil our electric kettle."

With that, out pours all of Dr. Gina's list. When

I stop, Carleen has my head on her shoulder. Cassie, the Snow Queen, seems unsympathetic.

"What are you gonna do?" cries Carleen. "You can't live with someone like that."

"But she's my mom!"

"Sounds to me like she's schizo or something. Blow your nose," Cassie barks.

I accept the tissue and wipe my face.

"Oh, Sylvie," sighs Carleen, "it's gonna be okay."

"I dunno about that," says Ryan from the doorway.

"How long have you been there?" asks Carleen.

"Long enough." He grabs a chair and straddles it. He is so close that I can see the pores on his nose. "Has this been going on for a while, Sylvie?"

Gulping, I nod. "A couple of years anyway."

"Getting worse though, huh? Does she know who you are? All the time?"

"Just sometimes."

He looks at me. Hard. "It could be Alzheimer."

"Old Timer's disease?" Carleen looks amazed.

"Can't be!" I sob. "She's only forty-four!"

"Don't call it Old Timer's disease, Carleen," Ryan says quietly. "It's not just old people who get it."

"What do you know about it?" I snap.

He takes a deep breath. "My grandmother has Alzheimer."

Grandma Anne, the tiny lady with the vacant eyes, the one who thought Ryan and I were dating again? But she was old! The thought of my mom becoming like … that …

"Maybe you should go home," says Cassie. "You're not much fun."

"If you do want to go, I could take you," Ryan offers.

"Yes, please," I whisper.

Just then, Trent bursts in, his eyes sparkling.

"Sylvie's going home," Cassie tells him.

"I'm taking her," Ryan adds.

"No way. I'll take her," Trent says, sticking out his chin.

Cassie places one slender arm around Trent's shoulders. "You should stay here. It's your house. Besides, I need to talk to you about the grad dance."

Trent flicks his eyes from me to Cassie and back again. "Oh, all right."

Ryan gets my jacket.

The cool night air wraps around me. I concentrate on trying to miss the biggest puddles of melting snow. That way I don't have to talk to Ryan. But he tries to talk to me.

"Trent is Cassie's boyfriend, more or less," he says as we stand at the bus stop. "Best you know that."

"Of course I know that. You're new here, not me!" I glare at him. He is illuminated by the street-light, smiling gently, sadly.

"Why'd you start hanging out with this bunch anyway? You're not like them. You're smart and ... and pretty."

My head jerks up to see if he's making fun of me. But he's peering down the street at the approaching bus.

"Trent and his friends are only interested in sports. Except Royce. He's okay. The others are just jerks or jocks."

"Which are you?" I counter. "A jerk or a jock?"

He tries not to laugh. "Neither, I hope. I'm kind of tired of the whole load of them." An uncomfortable pause before he says, "You going to grad?"

"Probably, but it doesn't seem that important anymore. And my piano exam is the same day. If I take it. Piano is one of those things I can't concentrate on right now."

The bus pulls up, and I stop Ryan from following me up the narrow steps. "No. I can get home all right from here. Thanks."

I quickly make my way to the far corner of the back seat, keeping my head down so my hair hides my face. As the bus moves off, I look through the back window. Ryan raises his hand in a wave.

Chapter Thirteen

The elevator mirror reveals smudged lipstick, black mascara streaks beneath my puffy eyes and messy hair. I spit on a tissue dug from my bag and scrub, but neither that nor the comb dragged through my hair makes much difference.

At the apartment I turn the doorhandle ever so gently and tiptoe in. The place is in darkness. Could she be asleep? I take baby steps toward my room.

A light clicks on. I freeze.

"Do you know what time it is, miss?"

"Dad! What are you doing here?"

I take in his appearance as he searches my face with cold eyes. His shirt is open at the neck and wrinkled. His pants show signs of being slept in.

"I'll ask the questions."

"Fine." I smirk. "It's 11:45."

"Don't use that tone with me. Where were you?"

"I told you I was going to Marissa's." I give my best jeez-parents-are-so-stupid shrug and roll my eyes.

"And what were you doing at Marissa's until this hour?"

"Playing Monopoly and Trivial Pursuit. She wouldn't let me go home until I lost. You know how she is."

"Yes, I know how she is," he said, crossing his arms. "She's just fine. I asked her when she called around ten-thirty wanting to talk to you. Care to try again?"

To stall for time, I about-face and march into my room, flipping on the light.

"So, let me guess," I snarl. "You're going to play the concerned father?"

"Sylvie! I *am* concerned."

"Ha! Nice try, Mr. I'm-Too-Busy." He can't argue with that!

We glare at each other, but I break first. He always could beat me in staring contests. "What happened with you and Mom? Where is she? Is she okay?" I collapse into the big armchair.

"She's in her bed, sleeping, I hope. But never mind about that now."

"Then how come you're here?" I'm annoyed at Marissa for phoning, annoyed at being caught.

"How come you're so interested in us all of a sudden?"

"How dare you speak to me like that!" He reaches me in two strides. "I *am* interested, a whole lot interested. I *am* your father —"

"Oh, you remembered."

I've never seen him so angry. Something must have riled him up long before I got home. Probably Mom. But his anger subsides and he sits on the edge of my bed.

"Where were you, Sylvie?" he asks, sounding weary. "Just tell me."

"I went to a party with some kids from school."

"A party, with boys?"

"Yes, of course with boys."

"Drugs or alcohol?"

"I didn't see any."

"Did you go alone?"

"Yes, but you know most of the kids. Remember Trent Thatcher?"

"Didn't he take MVP for North Kildonan in the Golden Boy Tournament back a few years?"

I should've known Dad wouldn't forget something like that. "He's been at school with me since kindergarten." I see a wary expression in his eyes. "There were lots of kids there. Some are really great." Carleen. Ryan. Especially Ryan.

"What are you doing tomorrow?" Dad asks. "I think we should have a talk."

I groan. "Do we have to?"

"Yes, we have to. This can't go on."

"*This?*"

"Oh, Sylvie, I knew something was wrong with your mom the moment I saw that dress. She always hated that shade of blue. The restaurant was a big mistake." He smiles sadly. "She kept asking what time it was. I couldn't keep her focused. She waved and smiled at complete strangers. It was almost impossible to have a regular conversation with her – but we did talk about you. I waited for you because ..." He lets the sentence drop. "Go to bed. If you hear grunting and swearing, it'll be me on that bloody uncomfortable couch."

"Tough."

He stops, takes a deep breath and looks at me over his shoulder. "We really need to talk. It's time you knew ... everything."

Chapter Fourteen

"The phone's for you," Mom shouts through my door. "Somebody called Marissa."

Somebody called Marissa? I don't remind her that Marissa has been hanging around our place forever. I force my eyes open and reluctantly pick up the extension.

"Jeez, Marissa. It's only quarter after nine."

"Good morning to you, too. I phoned last night to try to talk about what's left of our friendship but you weren't home. Where were you?"

"At a party."

"No way." She sounds hurt. "Care to enlighten me, your old pal, bosom buddy who, if you recall, you've been treating like dirt."

"Take a pill, Marissa," I snap. "Give me a chance to explain."

"Sure. Fine. I've been awake all night thinking up excuses for you."

"Will you be quiet!" I prop myself against the wall and start at the beginning. I don't leave out anything, not even Mom's dress or Dad's reaction when I got home late.

"So," she finally says. "Good-bye nice tidy life? And where do I fit in now?"

"Oh, don't be like that, Marissa."

"How else should I be? It's like all of a sudden I blinked and you were gone. Poof! One lost best friend."

"I'm still your best friend."

"Yeah, sure."

"You haven't exactly had time for me either."

"It's difficult."

"Difficult? Your mother?"

"I have to stick around home more and there's … things to do. But it wouldn't hurt you to phone me."

"We should've gone to the party together."

"Yeah, like I could have."

In my mind's eye, I see her sitting cross-legged on the cheap yellow linoleum in her dingy little kitchen. She even shares an airless basement room with her two little sisters. She needs something to cheer her up.

"Royce wanted to know why you didn't come."

"No way!" She sounds pleased, at last. But then

she covers the mouthpiece and shouts to someone. She whispers to me. "Listen, I gotta go. Mom wants her coffee. Right now. See you at school." As she hangs up, she screams, "It's coming, Mom. Give me a break!"

I put the receiver back slowly. Poor Marissa. She's so energetic, full of common sense. I've been lucky. Spoiled. And I'm a schmuck.

Mom is knocking on my door as she opens it. Her hair is combed in a ponytail. She has on a jean skirt and peasant top — and last night's diamond earrings. But her face seems bright and alert. She brandishes a spatula.

"Pancakes."

I throw on my pink housecoat — so frilly and childish — and tug open my curtains. Across the wind-whipped river, the trees of Kildonan Park are swaying and I think of the day I met Ryan on the footbridge in February. And about Grandma Anne, and Alzheimer. Mom *can't* have Alzheimer.

The scene in the kitchen could be mistaken for normal. Except that Dad hasn't been with us for breakfast for two years. He is reading the newspaper at the kitchen table. He needs a shave and is still in his rumpled pants and white shirt and looks tired. His syrupy plate has been pushed aside. Through the window behind him, buildings are black against the cloudy sky. He murmurs a good morning.

Mom sits across from Dad and smiles at her plate. Seven full-sized pancakes are being drowned in maple syrup.

"Hungry this morning, eh, Mom?"

Mom just digs in.

Dad looks up at her as she chews noisily, then at me, then back to his paper, but not before I see the deep furrow between his brows. It seems he isn't particularly eager to talk this morning.

I don't mention the sticky drip on Mom's chin. She seems to be enjoying her breakfast so much. The three pancakes on my plate are barely warm, but I eat them — the smell of pancakes gets me every time.

"Tea?" Mom asks, as if she's just been poked with a pin.

"No thanks," Dad replies. "I have coffee."

"I'll have some," I chirp, holding out my cup.

Mom pours some for me and for herself, stopping abruptly when her cup is half full. I can practically see the light going on in her mind. The urge to welcome her back is almost uncontrollable, but I pretend not to notice. She is obviously surprised to see Dad.

"Valli?"

He looks up from his paper. "I thought I should stay. You were ... well, I ..."

"This is like old times," she says. "I miss the old times."

Dad glances at me before smiling at Mom. "Me too."

I almost choke on my tea. He sounds like he actually means it.

Mom puts the teapot on its mat. "I need to talk to you, both of you, and seeing as how we're all together, we'd better do it now."

The pancake sticks in my throat. I swallow some tea.

She looks directly at each of us before continuing. "I believe that there is a problem with my memory or my mind. It's been going on for quite some time and I'm having trouble coping. I fade in and out. The only way I know I'm truly here is when I feel the overwhelming need to talk and be with people. I'm quite aware that these periods of reality are becoming fewer. And I can never tell when they will happen." She points to her plate. "Look at this heap. When would I ever eat so much for breakfast?"

She rises quickly and scrapes her plate ferociously over the garbage. Back at the table she takes my hand. "This must be dreadful for you."

"You'll get better, Mom. Dr. Gina is doing all those tests —"

"Please, it's as hard for me to say this as it is for you to hear. After all, it's *my* mind we're talking about. I'm looking forward to these tests because maybe they'll show something. But, sweetheart, they may not." Her eyes are glistening but her words are steady. "I don't think they will. I think I have ... what Celeste had. She was your great-grandmother. She lost her mind — I remember my mother telling me. It's a terrible thing to be locked up, Sylvie. And I can see myself getting worse with time."

I wrap my arms around Mom's neck. "Oh, Mom," I cry. "You said my name. You remembered."

She breaks down into huge sobs, and I cradle her head against my stupid frilly housecoat. Dad's so pale he looks gray.

"Have I forgotten who you are sometimes?" Mom weeps. "I'm so sorry."

"You can't help it."

"That doesn't matter," she argues. "It's terrible for you. And cruel."

"It's like you're some other person, a stranger, but still my mother." I blink against the tears. "I don't know what to do sometimes."

She gently unwraps my arms.

"Pay attention to what I'm going to say, because I don't know what I might say to you in the future." She uses her napkin to blow her nose and wipe her eyes. "I love you more than I have words for. You have always been a wonderful daughter. Your dad and I are very fortunate. We are so proud of you – how well you are doing at school and how ... responsible you are."

My cheeks flush as I think about my sliding grades, my lack of piano practice, my black vinyl jacket. I sniff loudly and try to concentrate as she turns to Dad.

"Is it possible for us, today, to deal with some legal issues? I don't want to be a burden to anyone. I want to check on my will." Her lips quiver. "And Dr. Gina did suggest working out the custody issue – while I still can."

"Custody? Wills? It sounds like you're going to die!" I wail.

"Sometimes I wish ..." she mutters.

I see her on the ladder on the balcony. "Don't say that!"

Dad pushes away from the table. "What kind of doctor tells a patient to get her affairs in order when nothing has been proven?"

"In this case, one who knows what she's doing, Valli. If it turns out that I have a fixable problem, what harm has been done?"

"I'll tell you what harm!" Dad bellows. "A child now thinks her mother is going to die!"

"Sylvie is not a child. That's why she's part of this discussion." Her hands tremble on mine. "I don't want her to be saddled with a woman who has a healthy body and an unhealthy mind."

"Marianne, please!"

"I want to get this thing wrapped up as soon as possible. I may not be functional for long." She looks back at me. "I want you to consider living with your dad if things get worse."

"No, Mom, no!"

"You may not have a choice." She looks from me to Dad and back. "And in case I am not myself when it is your junior prom in June or your birthday in August – damn, I don't know how else to say this. Your dad and I are planning to buy you gifts. He'll hold on to them. I might forget where they are." Mom puts her index finger under my chin and forces me to face her. "Sylvie, I don't really think I am fit to continue working. This sick leave can't go on forever. This weekend, I'm going to have to work up enough nerve to phone Tom Bartlet and quit."

"But you love your job!"

"Yes, Sylvie, I do," she says quietly. "But I can't teach. I can't control my students. I can't tell time

— numbers mean nothing to me. And I can't teach what I don't understand." She pauses for breath. "Things aren't right at home, either. Like that dress. I don't even remember buying it! That's pretty scary."

So that explains the squinting at the clock, the unread mail. I'm not sure I want to hear any more.

Dad's voice is thick. "We can look into your long-term disability plan and pension. And there's still the money I give you."

Mom's tears are dripping from her chin. "Consider living with your father, Sylvie. It's him or Grandmother Marchione, but she's not as well as she used to be — and she's in Toronto."

My heart splits down the middle.

"And, I want to say…" She pauses and bites her lip. "I … I want to say … happy fifteenth birthday, Sylvie, and congratulations on your graduation from … from …"

Her face goes blank.

Chapter Fifteen

The setting sun sends streamers of orange and pink through my window, but I hardly notice. I have spent a lot of time watching the bouncing triangles of my screen-saver. The apartment is quiet.

Mom and Dad have gone to a meeting downtown to deal with some of those legal matters Mom is so concerned about. And to have more tests.

It's been a month since that awful Saturday breakfast scene, and she's been "plugged in" less and less. Dad's been here – a lot. She's been confiding in him like suddenly he's her best friend. He says I have to talk to him – that I need to know the whole story. But I just want to talk to Mom. I want her to myself … while there's time.

They've had conversations long into the night – property, stocks, child support, health care, wills. They asked me several times to be part of the discussions, but I don't want to. I refuse to share in plan making, meals — anything to do with them.

Dad infuriates me. He's hardly had time for me these past two years. Now, here he is — trying to make it all better — hovering around Mom, catering to her every need, asking over and over if she forgives him for not being here for her. And she reassures him — over and over. He doesn't ask me, of course.

My garbage can is brimming with used tissues and crumpled essay attempts. I can't get a handle on math. My feeble attempts at B flat major and the sonatina turn into boring, stupid improvising until even I can't stand listening and find myself back in my room.

So, I sit beside the telephone, waiting for someone — anyone — to call. But who? Not Marissa, that's for sure. The ice is forming on our locker. Not Trent, not that it matters. He's tied so tight around Cassie's finger, it's amazing he can breathe. Not Ryan. Only his Grandma Anne thinks we're dating. Ryan and Trent had some kind of big fight after the party, and now they're not talking.

I hear the apartment door open. Reluctantly, mostly out of boredom, I saunter into the hall. Mom's bedroom door closes with a click before I can even say hello.

Dad is in the kitchen.

"How's Mom?"

"Lying down. She's tired from talking to Dr. Gina."

"Any more results from those tests she had before?"

"All normal."

"Good."

"But the psychiatric results aren't."

My heart gives a weird leap. "What's wrong with them?"

He's drying his hands on a towel as he walks around the counter. "The day you were with her, Dr. Gina did some preliminary evaluations."

"Yeah. Mom had to count backward from one hundred by sevens and weird stuff like that."

"She didn't do so great. Dr. Gina knew we were coming in for the tests today. So she had us in her office for a talk. Something is very wrong with your mom. I'm really worried."

My face tells him I'm not taken in by all his recent concern.

"Okay, Sylvie," he says. "We have to talk – about your Mom, about me and you, and what we're going to do."

"I've got homework."

"Well, the sooner we talk, the sooner you'll get

to your homework. I can stand here all night." He gestures to the living room. "Or we can sit."

"Fine." I flounce to the couch.

The yellowy brightness shining through the balcony doors lands on the film of dirt covering the coffee table. Dust motes float above the piano.

Dad takes a pink chair. "Your mom will always be important to me."

"And I'm supposed to believe that."

"It's the truth. Believe it or not." He rubs his face, stretching the skin. "And you are the most special person in my life."

"Oh, please." I can't help it – I laugh.

"You're gonna have to understand what went on in the past, because we'll have to work together in the future. Dr. Gina is pretty sure your mom has Alzheimer."

He hands me a blue and white pamphlet. I snatch it from his trembling fingers and open it. Only a few of the words sink in. As young as twenty-eight ... irreversible disorder ... language, memory, judgment, behavior and personality ... can be hereditary. *Hereditary?* I turn cold. If Mom has it – do I?

"Is Dr. Gina positive about this?"

"As positive as she can be. The only way you can know for sure is with an, um, autopsy."

"You mean Mom has to die before we'll know? I can't believe this!"

He gets up and walks to the window. "Because your mom's deterioration is rather rapid, Dr. Gina is testing for brain tumors and meningitis and any other possible cause for her ... problem."

"What happens now?"

"Well, unless it's one of those other things, she'll gradually get worse, more forgetful, more easily upset, unable to make decisions."

"She'll fade in and out, like she told us?"

"For a while. Then she'll ... she won't be your Mom anymore."

I want to cry but I can't.

"She was right, about sorting out her legal stuff?"

"Yes." His shoulders sag. "I will be your guardian until you are eighteen. I'll have power-of-attorney for her affairs."

A cold worm of horror snakes down my spine. "Will she ... get like Celeste? Will they lock her away?"

"People with Alzheimer aren't locked up anymore, honey, and from what I understand, she won't have to be placed in an ... an institution, as long as her family can handle her."

"That's me."

"That's *us*." He sits beside me on the couch. "I

have to talk to my boss about some time off, see about renting the house."

The words stick in my dry mouth. "It's going to be up to me to look after Mom?"

"Just until I can get some arrangements made." He takes my hand. His skin is warm and gentle, like it was when I was little. "Can you manage just a while longer?"

"I don't know. I can try."

He smiles. "That's my girl."

"I'm not your girl," I snarl, tugging my hand free. "You gave me up."

"I did not! I didn't want to leave. It was all your mother's idea."

"It was not! How can you say that?"

"Because it's the truth." He reaches for my hand again, but I move away. He sighs. "Your mother said she didn't love me anymore. Just one day, out of the blue, she says, 'Valli, I don't love you anymore. We never do anything together. We have nothing in common. We never communicate. I can't stand it. I want you to leave.' What was I supposed to do?"

"Fight!"

"Believe me, I fought. I wanted us to get marriage counseling, but she wouldn't go." His voice became quiet, deep, his bedtime-stories and making-jigsaw-puzzles voice. "I wanted joint custody, but your mother felt it best I only see you now and then. That was supposed to be less confusing for you. I never got used to not being with you."

I look at him sideways through narrowed eyes. "I don't believe you!"

He shakes his head and says, "I know how it must've looked." He peers into my face. "Would it help if I told you all the things that led up to the divorce?"

"Maybe later," I say. "Right now I have other things to worry about."

He follows me to the hall. "In the meantime, can your old dad have a hug?"

I hug him because it is easier than not hugging him.

I hear Mom's bedroom door click shut again. She's been listening.

"Sometimes I think she doesn't care about me anymore," I whisper.

"That's not true. Deep inside she cares."

"Yeah? How do I talk to deep inside?"

His answer is interrupted by the knocker — Mrs. Rathbone.

"Is everything all right, dear?" she asks, looking past Dad.

"Fine." I try to smile.

"I was wondering, you see, because I haven't

heard any piano for quite a while." She gives us both a sly smile.

"I've been busy with schoolwork," I reply quickly, avoiding Dad's eyes. He was always proud of my piano playing.

She seems relieved. "Oh, well, then, that's okay. I was hoping it wasn't because of, well, your mom. You know you can call on me any time if you need me. Good-bye, Sylvie, dear."

Dad follows her into the hallway. "Mrs. Rathbone, can I speak to you for a minute?"

The telephone rings and I grab it. Marissa's tone is cautious.

"I'm wondering how you're doing," she says.

It's great to hear her voice but her timing is awful.

"I hate us being mad at each other what with prom night coming. I've got this really cool dress." She sounds really sad. "And I could use a friendly ear."

"Yeah, well, I'm sorry. We're just getting ready for dinner. I gotta go."

"Okay but call me later. My life sucks."

I know I've let her down, but I can't help it.

Chapter Sixteen

I lie in bed, sick to my stomach, and not from eating too much. It's the spinning in my brain that's making me nauseous. Marissa sounds like she really needs to talk, but I just don't have the energy. I can't think straight anyhow. I should just sit and listen, but I can't handle much more.

Mom's in bed and the apartment is quiet. Dad has gone to his house, which is good. He makes me uncomfortable. I don't know how to fit him into my life now. It's simpler with him only on the fringes.

I promise myself I'll do a load of laundry before school tomorrow. I doubt that Mom notices the dirty clothes piling up. When I come home, I'll dust and vacuum. Maybe if I keep the apartment clean she'll be more relaxed.

I read and reread the pamphlet Dad got from Dr. Gina. There are some things I can do to make life easier — leave notes for Mom, keep her company. I can try to be patient and give her small tasks to do every day. We can go for walks in Kildonan Park now that summer is on its way.

I have to become a parent. I have to childproof the place. A teenage mother with a grown-up baby. I can do the banking and pay the bills as they come in. Dad wants me to try to keep up my life – and that includes piano. I'm going to have to call Mrs. Forrester. I haven't practiced.

The sound of shattering glass makes me leap out of bed. There are no lights on but I can hear Mom muttering in the dark bathroom.

"Mom! Are you –" I step on something sharp, and pain shoots through my big toe.

I grope for the light switch. Mom shields her eyes against the brightness. The drinking glass is in pieces on the floor.

I look at my toe. A large triangle of frosted glass protrudes from the bottom. Blood is seeping out around the edges. I know if I pull it out, a lot more blood will flow. I grab a towel. Mom reaches to help me.

"Don't move!" I order and she freezes. "Stay right there – until I get this glass out of my foot."

She whimpers like a baby.

Leaning against the doorframe, I yank the glass out of my throbbing toe. I wrap it as tightly as I can in the towel. "I'll get a broom. Now, don't move. Do you hear me? Don't move."

She nods, so I know she understands.

"Okay. That's good. Stay there."

I hobble to the closet, return with the broom and dustpan, and start sweeping.

Mom looks like she's going to faint.

"Put the lid down and sit on the toilet." She does, and sits cradling her head in her shaking hands.

The shards of broken glass grate together as I force them onto the dustpan.

"Why doesn't anything like this happen when Dad is here?" I mutter.

I hop to the garbage and let the glass slide in, put back the broom and dustpan, and get Mom's slippers from her room. She puts them on.

"Wrong feet, Mom!" I try not to sound exasperated.

I rummage through the medicine cabinet for a bandage while she figures out which slipper belongs on which foot. I find some gauze and the antiseptic. I wish Marissa was here. She knows first aid.

"Ow-ow-ow-ow," I moan as I dribble the antiseptic over the cut and slap on the gauze. I find some white tape, rip two long strips off and attach them to the gauze on my pulsating toe. Mom watches closely.

"What were you doing up anyhow?" I ask.

"Tea. Tea."

I bite back my frustration. "Let's make tea then," I say, hopping from the bathroom.

We sit and drink a whole pot of tea. When the dome clock chimes one-thirty, I say, "We've gotta go to bed."

"Not tired." She stares at her reflection in the window.

"What are you going to do at this time of night?"

"Not tired."

"I have to go to bed, Mom. I've got school tomorrow."

"Let's play cards."

"But it's so late ..."

"Please!"

"Oh, all right, one quick game." I lean back on my kitchen chair and open a drawer. I select a new deck of cards with Canada geese on the backs.

"Crazy eights."

"Not rummy? I thought it was your favorite?"

"Crazy eights!"

I lose count of how many times I have to tell her the rules. She cannot remember that eights can change the play to any suit or that aces mean you miss a turn. It's as though she's slipped even farther away. I work hard at my pledge of patience.

Finally, at three o'clock I give up.

"That's it. I've had it. You can stay here if you want but I'm going to bed." I kiss the top of her head. "Good night, Mom."

She doesn't reply, but picks up the deck and deals a game of solitaire, calling each card by name. "Queen of diamonds, nine of spades, three of hearts."

I crawl, exhausted, under my covers but toss and turn for the rest of the night. I can't sleep for Mom's voice reciting, over and over, the names of those cards.

When the alarm buzzes at seven, I angrily drag myself up and collect all my dirty clothes, empty the bathroom hamper, including the blood-streaked towel, and gather the dishcloths from the kitchen.

Mom is still playing solitaire, although she is quiet now. My anger evaporates. The two of diamonds is on the jack of hearts. None of the other cards line up properly either.

"How's it going, Mom?"

"Good," she replies. "I always win."

Chapter Seventeen

"You look awful! And you're limping!"

"Gee, thanks, Marissa." I drop my heavy binders into the metal locker. "You don't look so good yourself."

"Jasper has *another* ear infection. I was up all night with him in the rocking chair." She waves away her own problems. "What's with the leg?"

"It's not my leg. It's my big toe. I stepped on some broken glass."

"Ouch! Is it deep? Did you go to the hospital?"

"Nah, I fixed it up myself."

"Wonders never cease. So that's why you look tired?"

"No, I'm tired because I was up late playing cards with Mom."

"Five-thousand rummy, like at the lake last summer?" We both laugh.

"Hi, Sylvie." Ryan is plowing through the stream

of students. "How are you?"

"Good." I can't look at Marissa.

Ryan shuffles, obviously uncomfortable. "I have something here for you. My father says it's really good." He hands me a book with "Alzheimer" splashed across the cover. Then he's gone.

"Is there something you want to tell me?" Marissa asks. "That is, after all, Ryan Kostelniuk." She folds her arms. "Oh, never mind. I'm getting fed up with all your little secrets."

I don't want to fight. I change the topic. "Listen, how about coming shopping with me? I haven't got a dress for the dance."

"I figured you'd have bought some glamorous creation a long time ago."

I cringe, thinking of Mom's azure blue gown. "What's with you being so nasty all of a sudden?"

"What's with you leaving me out in the cold — for weeks now?"

"Come on, Marissa."

"Come on, nothing." Her singsong voice mimics me. "'*How about coming shopping with me?*' Puh-lease! You and I have been best friends for ... forever. But lately you don't even have time to talk to me." She looks hurt. "Seems you have lots of time for other people. Ryan obviously knows your problems. Such as they are." She catches her breath. "That sucks! Try walking a few miles in my shoes, sister!"

She turns on her heels and slams through the metal doors.

"Fine. I'll go shopping by myself then."

"No shouting in the halls, please," twitters Mrs. Kovacs. "Really, Sylvie! I don't know what's happening to you. You used to be so civilized."

I stare after her until she disappears into the office.

Chapter Eighteen

"I hope you had a good day, Sylvie dear." Mrs. Rathbone shuffles across the hallway as she does now every school day. "Your mom slept all morning. We played cards and watched TV for most of the afternoon. But we did go down to the store for my newspaper and cigarettes, and we talked to the girls in the hair salon. We sat out on the balcony awhile. She's not much of a talker, is she? Ah well." She sighs. "Oh, there's some lemon sponge cake on the counter for you from my supper last night."

"Thank you. Same time tomorrow?"

She nods. I smile and shut the door. The living room is strewn with newspapers. Dirty mugs and plates litter the end table. There's a trail of cake crumbs ending at a large squashed piece of cake ground into the carpet. Mom is channel surfing.

"Hi, Mom."

She turns off the TV and stands in front of me.

"How was your day?" I ask.

"Fine."

Fine? She used to go ballistic when I used that word.

"I think we need to clean up." I dig around in the broom closet for the spray cleaner. When I turn around, I bump into her. She's always following me around these days.

"Would you like to dust?" I hold out a rag.

She takes it and inspects it closely. I spray some liquid into the cloth. "Start with the coffee table."

I haul out the vacuum. As I snap the power head onto the handle, I work out my plan. After the place is tidy, we'll have an early supper and then go to the Corydon Avenue boutiques to check out dresses. If we don't have any luck there, we'll head to Kildonan Place tomorrow. Or Eaton Place on Thursday. No. Thursday is my piano lesson — if I go.

I drag the vacuum down the hall and attack the lemon crumbs. We need to move fast. The boutiques are open until six-thirty, but they don't appreciate someone waltzing in at six-fifteen, especially if that someone doesn't have a clue what she wants.

Mom slowly dusts one corner with irritating precision. Eventually, I grab the cloth and tell her to go make supper.

She stares vacantly at the kitchen. I realize that there is nothing thawing and nothing left over. I toss some bread onto the table, followed by peanut butter and strawberry jam.

"Make sandwiches, please," I command and finish vacuuming the living room at the speed of light. Every other room in the apartment needs cleaning, but they'll have to wait.

I attack Mom's sandwiches with the same vengeance as I did the cake trail. When we're getting ready to leave, Mom takes ages to tie her running shoes and comb her hair into a ponytail, but I do my best to smile and speak calmly.

The bus driver tells me it's five-thirty as he lets us off at the stop in front of Reena's House of Fashion. I run up the steps, with Mom at my heels. A little bell tinkles overhead as we rush in.

I feel as though I have stepped into the world of royalty, where ladies-in-waiting obey your tiniest wish. Wedding dresses dazzle me. Veils, head-dresses, tiaras, hats, ribbons and pins lie delicately in the glass display cases. Sprays of fabric flowers drape themselves over empty shelves. The light scent of roses wafts around us.

"Good afternoon." A plump saleslady approaches, her glasses dangling from a gold chain around her neck. She wears a pale green artist's smock. "Is there some special dress you have in mind, or are you just browsing?"

"I'm looking for a dress for my junior grad," I say, determined to enjoy this experience.

Her eyes sweep over my body. "Follow me, please. Remove your shoes, if you would. My name is Eadie."

We find ourselves facing a long row of dresses.

"Any idea what you might like?" she asks.

"No."

"Any particular color? Frills? Sleeves? Price range?

"Don't know."

She's a pro, hiding her impatience well. "Then let's take some shots in the dark." She rifles through the plastic-covered dresses, picking out four. "Go in there and strip down to your underwear. There's no need to be shy." She signals to Mom. "Why don't you sit over there."

Mom does as she is told, her expression as blank as one of Reena's mannequins. I wonder if bringing her was such a good idea.

"Here you are." Eadie comes into the change room with an armload of dresses. "Start with whichever you like best."

We work our way through several dresses but nothing seems quite right. Eadie's lips are getting tighter with each batch. In a controlled voice, she tries again.

"Those last three were average-priced dresses. This is a bit more expensive but it is very new." Eadie unwraps a short shiny black number, first the dress, then the lacy jacket. "Look closely at the colors within the material. When you move, there is a fine mauve and gray shimmer. See? Matches your eyes."

I see all right. I also see that it hugs my hips and exposes a lot of my legs.

"Very sophisticated, isn't it?" Eadie beams. "A nice pair of black pumps and maybe Mom's pearls or a simple necklace and you're set to dance the night away."

She checks her watch. "I hate to rush you, ladies, so would you like to think about it overnight, or ..." She lets the sentence hang.

I look over at Mom. She's in her own world.

"I'll take it."

"You're sure?" She casts a worried glance at the zombie posing as my mother. "Maybe you should discuss this first."

"No. She's given me the choice."

"Well, then, let's slip it off and box it for you." Eadie scurries to the front counter, my dress on her arm.

"Don't you love it, Mom?" I squeal, tugging my sweater down over my head. My hair crackles with static electricity.

I stick my face in hers and grin. She grins back.

"Let's buy it," I say, pulling her up and dragging her to the counter.

"Will that be cash or charge?" asks Eadie of Mom. Mom blinks stupidly.

"Oh, Mom," I say, poking her with my elbow. "Give me your purse."

I rummage through her purse until I find her wallet. She has twenty dollars and sixty-three cents. And no credit cards. Heat floods to my face. I never thought to check before we left the house.

"Is there a problem?" asks Eadie.

Sweat breaks out along my hairline and upper lip as I toss about in my mind for what to say, what to do.

Eadie inhales, long and slow. "Just as well I didn't ring it up."

"I'm sorry," I whisper. "This is so embarrassing. I'm so sorry."

"I could put it away for you, but only until tomorrow."

"No. Never mind. Thanks a lot. Come on, Mom."

I can't help it — I whimper and whine until we get home. Mom is oblivious.

"Tired, very tired," she says as she kicks her shoes off and drops her coat on the clear plastic protecting the welcome mat protecting the white linoleum. I have never understood that double-protection concept.

Mom goes to her bedroom without another word — no consolation, no sympathy, no nothing!

The answering machine is blinking. I push the button and listen.

"Hi, Marianne. Hi, Sylvie." Dad sounds tired. "Thought I'd phone you and see how you're both doing. Call me when you get in. Bye."

"Hello. This is Mrs. Forrester. I know we're taking this one week at a time, but I haven't heard from you, Sylvie. I'd appreciate a call this evening, if possible. Remember what we talked about! You know my number. Good-bye for now."

"Um, this is Ryan Kostelniuk, for Sylvie. My mom and dad wanted me to tell you that if — whenever you think you might want some help, you know, with your mom or to talk or whatever, to give them a call. The number is in the front of the book I gave you." Ryan's quiet, deep tone and his concern touch me.

I think about calling the Kostelniuks but change my mind. I don't know them — besides I'd rather talk to Ryan. As if! I call Dad. His line is busy.

The apartment is peaceful in the slanting evening sun, the river below a winding ribbon — but I'm restless. And tired. Tired of babysitting my mother, of trying to guess what she'll be like every time I walk through the door. I decide to quit moping and clean the rest of the apartment. Before I do that, I have a phone call to make.

"Hello, Mrs. Forrester, this is Sylvie."

"Ah, yes, hello, Sylvie." Her voice is warm, inviting. "I hope you're calling to say you'll be over tomorrow. These sporadic lessons aren't helping."

"Well, actually, no, I won't be."

Mrs. Forrester clicks her tongue. "I'm disappointed. I know you've had some difficulties. However, I had hoped you were over whatever it was. So I have to ask — are you giving up?"

I want to tell her to stuff her piano where the sun don't shine, but I'm not ready to be so final. "I'm not giving up, Mrs. Forrester. I told you I wouldn't have much time for practicing."

"Yes, you did. Does this mean that you will be here *next* week? Need I remind you that you still have three pieces to memorize? You're leaving it rather late, Sylvie."

I steady myself. "You're right. We'll try for next week. Bye."

I finish cleaning my bedroom and do the bathroom. Anything to pass the time. Ten o'clock comes and I don't feel much better. What I feel is depressed. I stand on the balcony, letting the breeze play with my hair. I can smell summer in the warm wind.

Mom comes out of her room in her housecoat and slippers, but I don't notice any nightie hemlines or pajama sleeves. Has she started sleeping in the nude?

"Play cards?"

"Oh, Mom. I was on my way to bed."

"Play cards, please."

"Okay, but just for a while." I reach for the Canada geese.

She opens the fridge and closes it again. She does the same with every cupboard.

"What are you looking for?"

"Food."

I pat a kitchen chair. "You sit. I'll make us some tea and toast while you shuffle. What are we gonna play?"

"Crazy eights."

I take a deep breath and explain that eights change the suit and aces mean you miss a turn.

Chapter Nineteen

Mr. Sisson corners me in the hall between afternoon classes three days later. "No more sluffing off. You've got some big tests coming."

"I know. I know." I work at not rolling my eyes. He's been on my case for weeks, making sure I've got my assignments in on time. I set my lips into a smile and prepare to launch into my usual arguments when I realize Mr. Sisson is looking over my shoulder. I swivel to see Marissa approaching our locker.

"Your face ... What ..." Mr. Sisson looks like he wants to throw up.

Marissa's left cheek is black and blue and her lip is puffy. She drops her hair forward in a feeble attempt to hide her bruises. I feel a knife turn in my chest.

"Hey, I walked into a cupboard door. It's so stupid. Don't look at me like that. I'm fine!"

She's lying. I know she's lying. Mr. Sisson knows she's lying.

"In my office, *now*!" he whispers hoarsely.

"Why?" Her voice is weak.

"You know why," he snaps. "I'll walk you there so you don't lose your way. Sylvie, tell Mrs. Kovacs that Marissa will not be in math this period."

"I want to stay with Marissa!" I state flatly. Marissa doesn't look at me.

Mr. Sisson gently pushes me aside. "Not right now!"

The buzzer goes, signaling time to go to class, but I barely move. No wonder she needed to talk. What a selfish bitch I am. I plod wearily up the stairs to face Mrs. Kovacs.

At three-thirty I stall at the lockers. Marissa doesn't show, but I can tell she hasn't been to the locker at all. I head to the Guidance office to find Mr. Sisson. I hear voices behind the closed door. I take a deep breath, gently turn the handle and open the door a crack.

"Marissa, for the last time, I can't let you go home," says Mr. Sisson.

"But I've gotta go," Marissa pleads. "My brothers and sisters —"

"We'll apprehend them immediately," says a female voice. "We are not allowed to return a child to an abusive situation."

I can just see through the small crack. Marissa is sitting between Mr. Sisson and a lady in a green suit.

"Mr. Sisson, may I have a word with you, please? Marissa, you stay here."

They move into the inner office. I slip onto a chair beside Marissa.

"Hey, Marissa! What's going on?" I whisper. "Are you okay?"

"Oh, Sylvie." Marissa drags a tissue across her eyes. "They won't listen. I'm trying to explain that Mom only ties one on occasionally now. She's been getting better, really. Besides, it's my fault that she hit me. I pissed her off – I wouldn't give her the keys to the truck. Usually she just goes for the parts of me nobody sees. I guess she was trying to improve my looks, eh?" Marissa gives a laugh wet with tears.

I want to take her in my arms. I want to take her home with me where she'll be safe and everything is normal. But everything is not normal at my house either.

"Poor little Jasper. Mom said he was crying too much, but he was only hungry. Usually I get up and give him a bottle as soon as I hear him, but I guess I was sleeping and didn't hear him until he started ... screaming. She was punching him on the side of the head. I should've heard him, at the first whim-per. I *always* hear him, Sylvie."

"What'd you do?"

"I got between her and Jasper." Tears roll down her cheeks.

I shake my head. I've known her forever and I still can't imagine her life. "Where's your dad? On the road?"

"Yeah, he's hauling between Toronto and Calgary." She swallows a sob. "Won't be back till tomorrow."

"Why didn't you tell me all this was happening?"

"Yeah, right! What do you think I've been trying to do – for months," Marissa snaps.

"You should've made me listen. Maybe I could've done something? We're friends."

"I'm not so sure we're real friends anymore. You don't seem to care about what is going on in my life. You shut me out."

"I did not!"

"Listen," she says, her lips tightening. "Maybe it would be better if we just gave up. I can't deal with your little problems at the moment."

"They're not little problems!"

"Oh, puh-lease," she sneers. "Is your mother beating the crap out of you? Are you eating maca-roni and cheese every night? Do you have seven people living in a two-bedroom house? Just go away, Sylvie. Go back to Cassie and Trent and your nice little parties." She stares defiantly. "Talk to me when you grow up."

I take off out of school and across the parking lot, almost knocking into Royce and Trent.

"Hey, Sylvie, hold up," Trent calls. "About the dance. We're gonna all sit together at the dinner. You'll be there?"

"Sure." I keep moving.

Royce shouts, "What about Marissa?"

"Ask her yourself."

Chapter Twenty

Mom is singing to herself as we walk into the grocery store and get a cart. She seems more like her old self. Maybe because it's June 4 — a beautiful Saturday morning and the weather is signaling summer.

We start at the deli counter, where she orders cooked ham, shaved not sliced, and some potato salad. I pick out some dark rye and pumpernickel. Mom trots merrily down aisle after aisle tossing tins, packages and boxes into the cart faster than I can add. I have to keep track. I don't have much money.

She is having such a great time that I haven't the heart to say anything. When she's checking the labels on cereal boxes, I take out some soup cans. When she is peering into the frozen food section, I sneak the third package of cookies back onto a shelf. People are trying not to stare at the nicely dressed lady and her weird daughter. Finally, I have to stop her.

"Mom, that's all we can get."

She blinks at me, puzzled. "What do you mean?"

"We can't afford to buy out the store."

"What?"

"Money? I only have so much money. I don't want a bunch of food in the cart when I can't pay for it."

"Pay for it?"

At last, I'm getting through. "Yes. Pay for it."

Before I can stop her, Mom is angrily unloading the groceries. She throws the cereal box across the aisle and kicks the tomato soup into the wheels of a passing cart. I wish I had let Dad come with us like he'd wanted. But no! I had to prove I could handle things.

"Mom! Stop it."

"What kind of place is this?" she screams.

"Mom, please. Be quiet. Stop right now!"

Cookies crumble beneath her heel.

"Is there a problem?" says a store employee. His name tag says "Harvey."

"You bet there is!" shouts Mom. "How come we have to pay for food? That's ridiculous. Isn't this a free country? Food should be free!"

A red-faced Harvey grabs the mozzarella before Mom can throw it at him.

"Now, ma'am," he says. "If you'll calm down,

I'm sure we can work all this out."

"What's to work out?"

"Mom, please." I tug at her sleeve.

"Let's get out of here," she says. "We can find food some other place."

I turn to Harvey. "I'm sorry. She's … not well."

"Why don't I take your cart and ring this up for you? You just keep a hold on your mother." He scurries the cart to the checkout, dispersing the crowd as he goes.

"Oh, Mom!" I growl. "Do you have any idea how embarrassing this is?"

"Well, it's a friggin' stupid country," she says, aiming her thoughts at a startled young woman. "We turn over vast quantities of our pay to the government. They're supposed to look after us. Well, I don't call this being looked after."

I drag her to the checkout.

"That'll be fifty-seven dollars and thirty-two cents," says Harvey. "I didn't charge for the damaged goods. Do you need help with your bags?"

"No." I hand over the money. "But I need help with my mother."

"Can't help you there. Have a nice day." He looks at Mom and then back to me. "Try to anyway."

"Now I know what it's like when your kid has a temper tantrum in public."

Harvey shakes his head and walks away.

"Move out, Mom," I order. I can't control the bitterness in my voice. "And no funny stuff."

She marches ahead of me, proud and defiant. I slink behind her to avoid eye contact with the other customers.

We get home and unload the groceries. I'm still fuming and hyper. She wants to sleep, but I convince her that going to the park would be good for her – fresh air would help her sleep better – at night. Before we can escape into the sunshine, the phone rings.

"Hello," I bark.

"Not a very nice greeting for your old dad. Did something happen?"

I leave out nothing. At least he doesn't say "I told you so." He asks to talk to Mom. It's not much of a conversation.

The sun blasts down on the Chief Peguis Trail Bridge. By the time we reach the gates to the park, we are sweating. We don't talk.

We turn down the main avenue of the park. Families are throwing Frisbees or baseballs, and a group of men are playing scrub soccer in the big open area. When we reach the flower gardens, Mom stops.

"Oh, look at the roses!"

The beds are bright with red, pink, orange, yellow, white.

"See, over here," she calls, and I go over. "How did they ever get a purple rose?"

We spend a long time admiring the gardens. I can see why she chose to have her wedding pictures taken on this hill.

"Hello, Sylvie." The soft voice makes me jump.

"Hey there, Ryan," I say, smiling widely, glad for the diversion. "What are you doing here?"

"Just walking."

He turns to the tiny woman with the glittering eyes beside him.

"This is my grandmother, Anne Kostelniuk," Ryan says. "Grandma, this is Sylvie Marchione."

I shake her outstretched hand. The fingers are cool and limp with a slight tremor. She gives no sign of meeting me before and barely smiles.

I interrupt Mom's examination of a Queen Elizabeth rose to do the introductions. After a brief hello, she stoops to smell a white John F. Kennedy bloom.

"Wanna walk with us?" offers Ryan.

"Sure. Come on, Mom. Let's walk some more, and then we'll go home for lunch."

She allows me to lead the way. Grandma Anne shuffles along at Ryan's side.

"She makes a rustling noise," I say.

Ryan lowers his head close to mine. "She can't control her bladder — it's her diaper."

"Gross," I say before I can stop myself, but I make a remarkable recovery. "Because of old age or the Alzheimer?"

"A bit of both probably. She's been like this for years. We bring her here every Saturday morning to give my grandfather a rest. Grandpa has asthma and arthritis, and finds taking care of Grandma Anne very tiring."

I search my mind for what little I know of Ryan to find something else to talk about. "So, do you like Winnipeg better than Saskatoon?"

He shrugs. "We've moved around so much, I try not to get too attached to any one place."

"But you keep leaving friends behind all the time, huh?"

"I guess." He takes the old woman's hand. "Keep moving, Grandma. Gotta get those legs pumping."

"I'm walking. I'm walking."

"She's in a bad mood today," he whispers.

I can't believe this conversation. Me and the high school hunk, out walking sick relatives on a bright June morning.

"How are things going with your mom? She seems pretty good."

She's standing on the footbridge, staring into space. "I have no idea what is going on in her head. Today she started throwing groceries around in Safeway because she found out we had to pay for them. She wants to play cards every night. Crazy eights! Over and over. And when I collapse into bed, she plays solitaire by her own rules, if she has any. She doesn't talk except to say hello and a word here and there. Other times she rambles on and on. Mostly she sits around or sleeps all day."

"Who looks after her while you're at school?"

"Mrs. Rathbone. She lives across the hall from us. Sometimes Dad takes time off work."

"Do you have someone to help with housework? Do you do it all by yourself?"

I shrug, but his brown eyes trap me and won't let me go until I answer. The word "clean" runs around in my brain. Ryan is clean and strong and well-dressed and kind and clean.

"I'm tired, Ryan," says Grandma. "Go home now."

"Okay, just a minute. Why don't you have a sit-down on that bench?"

The old woman lowers herself slowly onto the bench. Mom joins her. The sight of them brings tears to my eyes. They both wear the same blank expression that was on Mom's face as she perched on the balcony railing.

"She knows your name," I say.

"Yeah, she remembers mine – but not my dad's – and he's her son. And she doesn't remember anybody else except Grandpa. Your mom?"

"Nope. She called me 'daughter' for a while but not anymore." My voice breaks, and I look away. Ryan shakes his head.

"Grandpa says that some days he feels like killing her – and then himself."

"Oh! I can relate," I admit. "Usually I just want to shake her and shake her until I get my mom back. And sometimes she frustrates me so much I want to hit her. Of course, I don't – but I still feel guilty."

"If you need to talk, just call me. You've got my number." He peers anxiously into my face. "My grandfather says that the woman he loved and married is dead. The woman living in the house is a stranger he has to take care of."

"How can he think like that?" I cry. "She's his wife. That woman on the bench over there is still my mother. She's not dead."

"You've gotta let go."

"She's *not* dead!"

"I'm sorry. I didn't mean to upset you," he says softly. "Forget it." He goes over to the bench. "Come on, Grandma. Let's go. Nice to meet you,

Mrs. Marchione. Hope to see you again."

She waves gaily and watches as Ryan, Grandma Anne's hand in his, walks away.

I turn to Mom. "Why don't we go home and have lunch? I'm starving."

"Cooked ham on rye?" she asks hopefully.

"With hot mustard." I take her hand. Unlike Grandma Anne's, her grasp is warm and strong, and she returns my squeeze.

"Nice boy," she says.

Chapter Twenty-One

Several Saturdays go by before I decide to take a chance that Mom will not make a scene, and we walk to the market gardener's stall.

"Okay, Mom," I say as we wait for the red light to change. "I want to buy some flowers, and earth so we can plant them. But ... are you listening? I have to give them some money for the flowers. Okay?"

"Ridiculous!"

"Well, that's how it is, so don't give me a hard time, okay?"

"Ridiculous."

The stall is surrounded by shrubs, trees, rose bushes, flats of annuals and tables loaded with perennials. I have a sudden craving for growing things. I put two fake terra-cotta pots beside the cash register to wait. I don't want any more hanging baskets that might need fixing.

I spend ages trying to decide, and Mom is no

help whatsoever, so we emerge finally carrying two trays of mixed pansies. Because we are the one-hundredth customer, we are given a free trowel.

Back in the apartment, I set Mom to work mixing the earth and vermiculite with her new trowel while I gingerly climb up the stepladder and unhook the basket. I don't exhale until I am safely down. We plant, water and, after we've cleaned up our mess, share a glass of cola and admire our handiwork.

"Tiny people," she says. It takes me awhile to realize she's talking about the pansies. They do seem to have faces.

Mom is stretched out on the reclining chair. She looks ready to fall asleep. Her glass slips to a dangerous angle and I catch it just in time.

"That's it, Mom, have a nap. I think I'll tackle that sonatina."

I approach the piano slowly and reverently.

"I'm sorry," I say, caressing the smooth wood. "I'm here to see what I remember, if anything."

By the time I complete Hanon's sixth finger exercise, my wrists are sore. I am badly out of shape. I should be able to get to nine before the muscles in my arms tire. The triads and scales are not as demanding, and B flat gives me no trouble. I ace the sonatina the first time but can't seem to memorize it.

I open my notebook to read Mrs. Forrester's

comments from my last lesson and out falls a white slip of paper. "Exam – June 24 at 9:30 A.M. Please be there at least one half hour ahead to register."

June 24 is next Friday. I'm nowhere near ready.

I work for several hours, uninterrupted, on my three pieces and two studies, taking special care with dynamics and interpretation, until a sudden movement breaks my concentration. I stretch my neck to look through the glass door. The chair is empty.

The stepladder. Did I put it away? Is she on the top step, preparing to plunge to her death? I jump up from the bench, nearly toppling it, and rush to the balcony.

Mom is crouched in front of one of the terracotta pots, lovingly touching the velvety petals of a pansy. Only when she turns and smiles at me does my stomach unknot. The stepladder is leaning against the wall, folded, unthreatening.

Out loud I say, "Our next place will be on the main floor."

I'm still shaking fifteen minutes later. Fortunately, Mrs. Rathbone is home and willing to stay with Mom while I go for a walk. I promise to be back within half an hour.

I stride down the sidewalk – my mind in a whirl, my eyes barely focused – until a flash of color in a shop window stops me.

I take four steps backward and find myself in

front of a short deep purple dress and matching jacket. It's not quite the same cut as the one in Reena's, and the material is different.

I squint up at the sign. "What Goes Around, Comes Around. A Used Clothing Boutique."

A secondhand shop! I've never even been in one — the idea's kind of strange. But the dress is calling me and I push open the heavy door.

This place sure isn't Reena's — dark, packed with clothes of all descriptions and colors, cheap plastic flowers on the counter, a musty smell hovering over the place.

Someone appears from behind a curtain at the end of the shop.

"Hi, Sylvie. What can I do for you?" she says in a surprisingly pleasant voice.

"Jen? What are you doing here?"

"My mother owns the place. She's on a break."

"Oh! Can I see that dress?"

"The purple one? Awesome. You wanna try it on?" She reaches into the window display and unhooks the hanger.

"What size is it?" I ask, holding my breath.

"Don't even have to look," she says. "It'll fit. Try it on."

The dressing room is a cubicle with hardly enough room to turn. There is no mirror, but at least I don't have to parade around in my undies.

"If you want a mirror," she hollers through the ugly curtain, "it's down by the fur coats."

The dress slips on like a dream and I go to check it out in the mirror.

"Fabulous," she says. "Thirty bucks."

My jaw drops. She holds up her hand.

"Know what you're thinking. You come into a secondhand shop, and we should be giving the things away. But our top items are on consignment. People need a little return on the clothes they paid too much for in the first place."

"Oh, I'm not arguing with the price," I say, strutting in front of the mirror. "It's just ..."

"Don't tell me," she says, leaning on a rack of mink jackets. "It's the idea of wearing a used dress."

"Well ... yeah."

"Been there, done that. You'd be surprised at who shops here!"

I blink. "Really? Like who?"

She wiggles her eyebrows. "My lips are sealed."

I figure she's talking about Cassie and Carleen.

"I'll take it," I say. "Can you hold it for me?"

"Only until tomorrow at closing time."

"Do you take trades?"

She purses her lips. "Like what?"

"My black vinyl jacket?"

"Awesome!"

I hold out my hand. Grinning, she shakes it.

A warm breeze lifts my hair. I'm sitting on Mom's chair on the balcony, studying. My eyes hurt. My head hurts worse. Dad slides open the glass door, steps out and breathes deeply.

"Supper was good, Dad."

He chuckles. "You're just happy you didn't have to make it. Bet you miss your mom's fancy cooking, eh? Me too."

I shrug and we're quiet for a while, lost in our own thoughts.

He flips through one of my textbooks. "Anything I can help you with?"

"Don't think so. I'm as ready as I'll ever be."

"I can't believe you're graduating." He winks. "Next year, senior high school."

I send him a little smile. I'm getting used to him being around.

He returns my smile. "Are you gonna do your piano exam? Think you can pull it off?"

"Hopefully."

"I'll drive you there if you like. We can ask Mrs. Rathbone to keep an eye on your mom." He stretches his legs. "Boy, the view from here is great. Perfect for talking."

I take the hint and put down my history notes. "So, Dad, how's work?"

He scratches his head. "Work's work. This job site is a problem, though. I hate building on land-filled swamp." He gazes up at the sky. "You know, when I first met your mother, I thought she was the most exciting woman in the world. And the most gorgeous. She had an opinion about everything. Then about three years ago she started to change." He sighs. "I didn't know then what I know now, but when I think back ... well, there were signs even then. Maybe it was unkind of me, but I used to tell her she had a memory like a sieve. She'd tell me something one day, and the next tell me something completely different. And the long silences. The drifting off into space. The mind games."

"You thought she was nuts?"

"No, not nuts. I didn't know *what* was going on. I figured she couldn't stand the sight of me, and this was her way of dealing with it. I was hurt at first. Then just plain angry. And suddenly, it was bye-bye, Valli."

"So, you walked out and left me behind?"

His face hardened. "She insisted a girl should be with her mother. I tried to see you as much as possible, but I think she was afraid she'd lose you to me. I had to beg to see you. Do you know how many times I called you last year to try to set up a visit?"

"How many?"

"My lawyer said I should keep track, so I did. One hundred and four. That's twice a week. Oh, I'd get a hold of you now and then, but most of the time Marianne would manage to intercept. I have no proof, but I'd bet she was erasing my phone messages before you heard them and not telling you I called. I can count our visits on one hand. She'd even tell me I could see you, and then, when you didn't show at the burger place, I'd phone and she'd claim not to know what I was talking about. She let you go on believing I —"

I stand up, toppling the chair. "I don't want to hear this, Dad. I get the picture."

"I'm sorry, honey," he says softly. "I'm being self-ish, but I'm tired of being the bad guy in the story."

"So, Mom's the bad guy!"

"No. I'm willing to accept my share of the blame. And now it's obvious she wasn't … herself. Look, I just thought that with your mom going downhill so quickly, it was time for everything to be out in the open. And you've been avoiding it." He gets up and puts his hands beside mine on the balcony railing. "I'm sorry this hurts so much."

I can't look at him. I keep my eyes on the river, swallow the painful lump in my throat.

"I'll be going," he says wearily. "Unless you'd like me to stay?"

I shake my head, not trusting my voice.

"Your mom is channel surfing. She's pretty tired. Maybe you'll both get a good night's sleep tonight." He slides open the glass door. "I'll call you tomorrow and be over in the evening."

When the apartment door closes, I throw myself down into my chair. He *can't* be telling the truth. Mom would never do the things he accuses her of. He's blaming Alzheimer for their marriage breaking up, for her personality changes – years ago. Well, there's one way to find out if that's possible.

I pull the book Ryan gave me out from under my history text and start reading. It doesn't take long. Dad may not be lying. Mom is on every page. And if I'm honest with myself, she has been *very* possessive of me the past few years. Possessive but less and less aware of what I'm doing or not doing.

If, as Dad says, it's time to get everything out in the open, then I want to talk to someone. Marissa is right. We need each other. I was just too wrapped up in myself to understand. Tomorrow I'll wait for her at the locker – and listen, not just talk.

Chapter Twenty-Two

I catch up with Marissa after the French exam on Monday.

"That was a tough one."

"Midterm was harder," she replies. "Hey, I'm not going to run away. You can let go!"

"I'm not so sure."

"What?" she retorts. "That the midterm was harder or that I'm not going to run away?"

"Both."

From this angle I can just see the very pale yellow remains of her mother's beating. My insides roll over. She takes a step toward our locker.

"Marissa, stop. Look …" I don't know where to start. "Listen …"

"Crossing the street?"

"What?"

"You know, stop, look and listen." She rolls her eyes. "Honestly, sometimes you have no sense of humor."

"How can you even think about humor?" I cry. "You were right. I need you. We need each other ... I hope. I can't stand this not being friends."

Her eyes narrow. "Yeah, I suppose it is time to clear all this up. We've been friends almost our whole lives. Besides, I'd rather not spend my nights thinking about how much I miss you. Let's go to study hall and talk." She starts toward the area set up for students who want to do homework during spare periods.

Royce comes bounding up behind us.

"Marissa. Marissa!"

I fade back against the lockers. She looks at me, puzzled.

Royce fidgets and seems uncomfortable. His dark hair and eyes reflect the fluorescent light.

"Hey, Royce, what's up?" Marissa keeps her bruised cheek turned slightly away from him.

"You going to the dance? Wanna sit with me?"

"Oh, Royce, I don't know ..." Her shoulders slump. "I wasn't going to go."

"Yeah, well, I can understand that," he says, deflated. "See ya –"

"But, hey, you convinced me – sure, why not."

He trots off down the hall, grinning broadly. We break into giggles. It's like being back in elementary school. I've missed her so much.

"Marissa, I want to apologize. If I'd only been paying attention, I'd have —"

"Yeah, yeah," she replies, "but I wasn't being particularly understanding either, of … your mom and all."

"Is Jasper okay? Is your father home now?"

"We spent the first night in a safe house. The people were nice. But it was awful — the kids refused to sleep unless we were all in the same room. Both sisters insisted on coming with me into the bathroom. The boys were terrified we'd be split up. Jasper cried all night."

"What about your mom?"

"I don't know. She's locked up somewhere waiting to get into a place to get dried out. I haven't seen her. Then, the next day, my dad came and got us and took us home. He was so upset, blames himself. Says he figured shit like this was going down. His exact words. He's filing for custody, of course. Know any good lawyers?"

"My dad might."

Chapter Twenty-Three

I stare at Mom as she sleeps. I'm ready to go to my piano exam. Mrs. Rathbone is due to knock at the door any minute. The past four days have been scary with all the school tests and exciting with all the grad preparations. I'm flooded with the urge to talk. I sit on the edge of the bed and take her hand.

"I miss you." I take a deep breath. "I really think you tried to kill yourself on the balcony that day. Of course, I can't say for sure. I tried to talk to you and you got really angry. Now I don't think you're able to tell me anything except that I should live with Dad. He's been here a lot. Sometimes you freak him out.

"Dad keeps trying to make conversation but you don't seem to 'see' him. It's like he's a ghost you pretend isn't there. Actually, you're like that with me too, more and more. You get unplugged a lot but it's worse than before. You can't get your words out, or you keep repeating the same word over and over.

"Dad said you were the one who wanted out of the marriage. Why didn't you just tell me? I'd have understood, eventually."

Mom's chest rises and falls. Her mouth parts slightly as she moves her head toward me. I fool myself into thinking she's actually listening.

"I hope you'll be okay at the presentation this afternoon. This thing that's wrong with you, I don't want it wrecking my special day. You'll just have to stay with Dad.

"I don't know who you are anymore. It is like Ryan's grandfather said, about his wife being dead. But a dead person is gone, buried. And you're not dead. I don't want to believe that some stranger, who looks like my mom, has moved in.

"Oh, Mom, I miss you. I miss the way you were always nagging me to keep up with my schoolwork, and I miss the fact that supper would always be made. I miss you laughing. I even miss you arguing, and I never thought I'd ever say that!

"I'm so tired. By ten o'clock most nights I can hardly keep my eyes open. I try to convince you to go to bed but you won't. I try to undress you but you bat at my hands and run from room to room. You won't put on your pajamas until I put on mine. Then you want to play cards.

"If I have to explain the rules for crazy eights one more time I'm going to strangle you. No, I didn't mean that! I kiss the top of your head like you used to do to me and leave you sitting at the kitchen table with a cup of herbal tea.

"While I try to fall asleep, I hear you walking around the apartment, going to the bathroom, opening and closing cupboards. One night you rattled the handle on the front door, probably making sure it was locked. And it's usually getting light before you get to sleep – and start snoring, I might add.

"At least my piano exam will be over soon. Mrs. Forrester will be so happy. I'm glad I'm doing it, but I'm nervous. Doesn't matter if I pass or fail ... well, sure it does. I hate failing. I know I passed all my school exams, but I don't think by much.

"And tonight is the dance. I can't wait to show you my dress. Whoever gave it to Jen's mom's store hardly wore it. It looks and feels like new. It's going to be fun tonight. I can't wait to," my voice drops away as I look at her peaceful face, "tell you all about it."

I kiss her softly on the forehead. She stirs but doesn't wake.

ക്കക്കക

"It's going to be one hot Friday morning with barely
a breeze from the southwest and an approaching
weather disturbance –"

Dad turns off the radio.

My stomach tingles with nerves. The traffic is
moving at a crawl.

Impatient, Dad goes through a yellow light and
up University Crescent to the music building. He
drops me off and says he'll pick me up after the
exam. I grab my music case and run.

The heat presses in on me. My thin cotton dress
sticks to my legs as I climb the stone steps. I can't
wait to reach the cool, dark halls, where I can catch
my breath.

Mrs. Forrester, crisp in her white blouse and
blue skirt, sits chatting with the registrar. They
both smile as I come toward them, the sound of my
heels echoing. Strains of piano music escape from
behind one of the heavy wooden doors to my right.
The place is dark but it's not cool.

"Here she is!" cries Mrs. Forrester. "This is my
student, Sylvie Marchione."

"Have a seat, Sylvie," says the registrar as I hand
over my slip of paper. "You are next, as you may
have guessed."

Mrs. Forrester pats my hand as I sit beside her.

"I am so glad you're here," she says. "I couldn't sleep last night worrying that you might change your mind and not show up. Don't worry that you weren't able to memorize all of your pieces perfectly. You know you can use your book if it means you will make less errors. You'll lose a few marks but, if you play as well as you did yesterday, you'll do more than fine."

She reaches behind her chair and produces a brightly wrapped gift.

"This is for you, to show you how pleased I am with your progress – and how proud I am of you. I want to give it to you now so that whatever happens in there," she says, pointing to the door, "and whatever you decide afterward regarding your piano, you'll always have this to remind yourself of the day you took this big step toward maturity. You can open it if you like. Or you can wait."

"I'm going to wait." I can barely swallow, my mouth is so dry. My leg starts to jiggle.

Mrs. Forrester smiles. "Getting focused?"

I nod, afraid to speak in case my voice quivers.

The door opens and out walks a boy about twelve years old. He is followed by an elderly gentleman wearing a three-piece suit.

"Well done, Elliot. Keep up the good work," he says. "Now, who's next?"

"This is Sylvie Marchione," answers the registrar.

"Come in, Ms. Marchione," he says with a sweep of his arm.

I hear Mrs. Forrester say to the registrar, "I always accompany my students to their exam. It's as much a test of my skill as it is of theirs."

The elderly gentleman closes the door and shakes my hand.

"I'm George Andersen. Please take your place at the piano."

I wipe my hands on my dress as I sit in front of the Yamaha grand. My palms are wet. My underarms are prickling. My heart is hammering in my chest. I'd love a drink of water like the one George Andersen has on his table.

"Have you taken any previous examinations of this kind?"

"Yes, sir."

"Good. Then you know the rules, but I'll review them anyway," he says. "As much as possible from memory. No retry or restart unless you or I expressly ask for one. No questions except for clarification of my instructions, and, of course, no second endings. We shall do the technical requirements first. Are you ready?"

"Yes, sir."

"The scale of B flat major ..."

Somewhere after he says "no questions" my brain goes into neutral, but the musician in me surfaces. My books never leave my case. I don't retry or restart anything. I ask no questions and don't do any second endings. Unfortunately, I don't think I give the pieces any emotion, and I mess up on some dominant and diminished chords, but I walk out with my head held high.

"Well done, Sylvie," George Andersen says, clamping his sweaty hand on my sweaty shoulder. "Keep up the good work."

Only then does the haze lift, and I rush over to Mrs. Forrester.

"I survived!" I unwrap the present to find a book called *Chopin's Most Loved Musical Pieces*. "Thank you, Mrs. Forrester. It's very kind of you after what I've put you through these last few months."

"You put *me* through nothing," she says. "You put *yourself* through it. The book may be a bit advanced for you but someday …"

"Maybe!"

"How about we have some iced tea to celebrate?" she asks as we make our way out into the white brightness and oppressive heat.

"Can't, but thank you. I have to get home. It's my grad this afternoon."

"Oh, of course. Congratulations on your graduation, my dear." She holds me at arm's length. "I can only hope I'll see you again in the fall, Sylvie, and that everything is getting back to normal at home."

"We'll see what happens over the summer," I reply. "Good-bye, and thanks again for the book and … everything."

I run, not looking back. What a relief! It's over. Now I don't feel like a quitter. And, for a while at least, no more piano!

Dad has the air conditioning in the car cranked to max. He asks about the exam.

"I did it. Let's just get out of here."

Back at the apartment, Mrs. Rathbone is reading the newspaper at the kitchen table. Dad winks at her. She pretends to ignore him.

"Your exam, how did it go?"

"It went okay. Thanks for asking."

"I can't tell you how delighted I was when I heard you practicing these last two days," she says and then blows her nose.

I tilt my head sideways. "You don't look too good!"

"Summer cold. My sinuses are all plugged up." A grin splits her face. "Say, it's your graduation today, isn't it, dear? Need me to look after Mom?"

Dad pipes up. "No, it's okay. I'm going to stick around. You really look awful."

"Thanks a lot," she says. "But no problem. Let me know if you need me."

I gently close the door.

"I'll check on Marianne," Dad offers. "She can't *still* be sleeping. Maybe we can all have lunch together. Okay with you?" He sends me a questioning smile as he heads for Mom's room.

"I guess so." With a heartfelt sigh, I sink into a wingback and enjoy the view through the glass door. A sparrow is sitting on the balcony railing. Its feathers are buffeted by the strong breeze.

"Sylvie, come quick!" Dad's voice is panicky. "Did Mom have any sleeping pills?"

I rush to the bedroom and brush by him. "I don't know. Why?"

"I can't seem to wake her."

"Mom! Mom!" She's so still. Her breathing is very shallow. I shake her.

"I tried that," says Dad. His eyes spark with fear.

"Did you find any bottles or anything?" I ask. He immediately starts searching the messy room.

I stare down at her pale face. "I never should have left without making sure she was awake, but she was sleeping so peacefully and I was in a rush to meet you downstairs. What if —"

"Here it is, in the drawer," he says, holding up a small container — extra-strength painkillers. So, she managed to get the lid off this time. I grab the bottle from his fingers. There's only one pill — stuck to the bottom.

"Sylvie," Dad says, his voice icy, "you really must pay more attention."

I gasp, torn between insult and rage. I'm about to argue when Mom groans and moves her head. Slowly she opens her eyes, but when she sees us frowning down at her, she grabs the duvet and shrieks with terror.

"It's okay, Mom, relax," I soothe. "We are not going to hurt you."

"My God, Marianne," Dad says, "you scared us."

"Mom, it's me."

Her blue eyes are wide with fright as she looks at us over the comforter. Impulsively, I throw my arms around her neck, hugging her, hugging my terror away.

"Come on, Mom. Get up."

A thin white hand shoots out toward the night table, searching.

"We've got the pill bottle, Marianne," Dad says. "How could you do this? What were you thinking?"

She looks at him like he's a three-eyed alien from another planet.

"No! No!" she repeats, over and over. "No! No!"

Dad reaches for her. "This isn't the answer."

"No! No!" She pushes him away and swings her legs over the far side of the bed.

"Leave her alone." I crawl over the bed to take her in my arms. I brush the sweaty hair off her forehead. "We don't know for sure she tried anything."

Dad gives an exasperated sigh. "We don't know she didn't."

"She probably had another headache," I suggest. "She took some of these last time."

"Did she sleep this long last time?" he barks. "Have you any idea how many pills were in this bottle when she decided to take them *this* time?"

Mom suddenly gets to her feet. "Get dressed," she says in a funny, otherworldly voice.

Dad tries again. "Marianne, how many pills did you take? Did you deliberately take too many?"

"No! No! Get dressed." Mom starts pacing across the small room, biting her fingernails and giving Dad that blank look.

For a brief moment, I believe her. I'm filled with belief that her repeated 'No's mean she didn't take too many pills, that she hadn't been going to jump off the balcony, that she knows what she's doing.

Ready to defend her if she gives me even the slightest sign, I step in front of her and pull her hands away from her face. But her blank eyes drill into my soul. She hasn't a clue who I am or what she's doing. Nothing has changed — except maybe she's worse.

She backs into the corner of her dresser. "Get dressed."

I swallow my pain. "That's right, Mom. Get dressed. Something cool. It's hot outside. Come on, Dad. She'll be fine now."

He eyes her suspiciously. "We're right outside the door if you need anything."

In the hallway, he wipes a hand across his brow. "Man, that scared me."

I think about his earlier comment — about me being more careful — and my tone takes on an edge. "Now you know what I have to live with all day and all night. You never get used to it."

His mouth opens and closes like a goldfish while he tries to find the right words. For effect, I drop the pill bottle dramatically into the garbage and retreat to my room. I can hear him trying to persuade Mom to drink some instant coffee. She keeps repeating that she wants tea and that she wants him to go away. Eventually, he does. I hear the sliding door open and I know he's getting some air.

I can't push the depressing episode from my mind. I stare at the purple dress hanging on my closet door. The material is cool and smooth to my fingertips. It's beautiful — but I can't wear it. I can't go out. Not now! Not with Mom the way she is! She really *is* getting worse, and there's nothing I can do about it — except maybe spend more time with her. Try to keep her calm. I decide to tell Dad he can go to work. I'm staying home. I march down the hallway, my mind made up.

Mom is pacing on the balcony. If there was a stepladder, would she jump?

"I can't get her to sit down," Dad says before I can say anything.

I bite my lip. "I'm sure she knows — somehow — that this is an important day."

Dad looks helpless. "I figure she can't get her mind around what her heart is feeling."

Mom comes over to me. Her hair is plastered to her head, and she has wet spots under each arm and around the neck of her sundress. She looks into my eyes and seems to want to say something. I give her a small hug.

Dad takes his turn, pressing me tightly to his chest. His eyes are bright with emotion, his mouth trembling.

"Sylvie, I am very proud of you."

I can't answer – can't say what I came to say. The tears are too close.

"Your mom and I have some presents for you." He indicates for me to sit in a chair. Mom perches on the arm beside me.

"This is from your Mamma Marchione." Dad hands me an envelope.

I tear it open to find a card and serious cash. "Wow!"

"And this is from us." He slips a brushed velvet case into Mom's hand, and together they present it to me.

I run my fingers along it before popping the lid. The gold locket and chain lie elegantly on the black velvet. I pry it open. One side holds a photo of Mom and Dad, their heads touching, both very happy. The other side is empty.

"What's wrong?" asks Dad. "Don't you like it?"

"It's beautiful," I mutter.

"So, why so sad?"

I take a deep breath and stand up. "I'm not going to grad. I'm staying here. With you guys."

Dad's eyebrows shoot up. "What are you talking about? Of course, you're going. There's the awards ceremony and then the big dance later. You don't want to spend tonight with a couple of old fogies like us."

"Yes, I do." I nod emphatically. "I've made up my mind." My eyes flick to Mom, who is biting her nails again.

Dad puts his hand on my shoulder. "I know what you're doing and you don't have to. Mom will be just fine. She would never want you to stay home because of her."

My chin comes up. "Well, I'm staying home anyway. We'll play crazy eights or something."

He peers into my eyes. "Sylvie, that's very good of you. But," he pauses, "you don't really want to stay home. Not really. Not tonight. What about Marissa? And Trent Thatcher? What about all the other boys waiting to dance with my beautiful daughter? What about you having some fun for a change. You certainly deserve it." He senses my resolve beginning to crumble. He smiles. "Tonight's your night. Go get dressed."

Mom is at my side. "Get dressed. Get dressed."

I know she's only repeating what she said in her room earlier, but I choose to think she's encouraging me.

I give them hugs and thank yous, pretending I live in a normal family, and escape to my room before I cry and end up with my face all red and splotchy. By the time I shower, dress and slip into the slightly too-high heels, I feel a bit better. Dad can manage. And he's not going anywhere. I can relax, go to the dance and enjoy myself — something I haven't done in ages. I put on my mascara and lipstick — a slightly less radical shade than I've been wearing these past few months — and burst into the living room for approval.

Chapter Twenty-Four

The school air conditioning is powerless against a gymnasium full of sweaty bodies. I spy my mom and dad sitting near the back. Mom is smiling. She looks almost like an ordinary mother, but I can tell she's restless, ready to bolt or start shouting. Dad waves.

Marissa is beside me like she has been for years. She looks beautiful in pink. Trent, Cassie and the others are all together, near the front. I can only see the backs of their heads. Ryan is two seats over, in my row.

"Your mom looks great," he says, holding my gaze, unsmiling, until I feel my cheeks burn.

"And now for our special awards," says Mr. Gregory, taking his position at the podium very seriously, "given to those students who displayed outstanding self-discipline and intellectual effort in each subject. First, the award for athletics. To win this award, a student must have an intelligent, mature attitude to all sports and maintain a higher-than-average grade point. Apart from this, the student has to be an all-round great person. Ladies and gentlemen, it gives me great pleasure to award this honor to – Royce Martin, captain of the basketball team."

Loud whooping and hollering and much applause later, Mr. Gregory works his way through all the awards except the one for mathematics.

"This year, as you know, marks the retirement of Mrs. Kovacs. And while the school isn't going to be the same without her, she will stay with us in spirit. It is her wish that a scholarship fund be set up in her late husband's name to help a student to continue developing his or her mathematics skills at an institute of higher learning. We honor her this year by inaugurating this award. Mrs. Kovacs, this podium is yours."

Mrs. Kovacs hobbles to the front of the stage. "I've been at this high school for far too many years. But over the last few of them, I have been delighted to see an increasing emphasis on mathematics in the curriculum. We teachers always knew it was important, but now the students are realizing, too – that's what really counts. Anyway, the recipient of the Neil Kovacs Memorial Award for extraordinary achievement in mathematics has to have shown a consistent eagerness for all aspects of the subject, be in the top ten percent on all tests and exams, have regular attendance and brush his or her teeth every morning."

The hall erupts with laughter. "Just checking to see if anyone was listening. The last part really reads 'and behaves in accordance with school regulations.' I think everyone must know who is going to be the very first recipient of the Neil Kovacs Scholarship. And I am delighted. Sylvie Marchione."

I gasp.

Marissa squeals and flings herself at me. "Way to go, Sylvie!"

Kids are playfully knocking me on the back. Ryan gives me an excellent grin. I notice Cassie roll her eyes. Trent gives me the thumbs up.

Mrs. Kovacs is smiling lovingly at me. I try to look poised and grateful when she hands me an envelope and a scroll before shaking my hand. She smells of lilacs.

She says, "Do something with your life. Or else I'll find you and cause you grievous bodily harm."

"Thank you." I chuckle and bow. I have to pose with Mrs. Kovacs for Dad and his camera before I am allowed off the stage.

The parade for diplomas starts and the heat

increases with every passing second. The ceremony seems to take forever, but at last it's over and we find ourselves out in the glaring sunshine while caterers and janitors set up the gym for dinner.

Around me, Marissa, Royce, Carleen and Jen chatter like a bunch of squirrels. Trent's voice is the loudest, making rude remarks about the teachers and saying how glad he is to be moving to a new school, where the teachers don't know him and might give him a break. Marissa and Royce are smiling at each other. Marissa is fiddling with her program and Royce doesn't seem to know what to do, so he stuffs his hands in his pockets.

Trent is giving me a headache. I wish I knew how to shut him up.

Cassie saunters across the lawn. I wonder if she got her tight royal blue dress from Jen. I grin at the thought. She deigns to nod slightly as she puts one elegant hand on Trent's arm.

"Enough already," she says. "You're acting like an idiot."

His energy drains as if she pulled out a plug. Just like Mom's energy drains.

"I see your parents aren't here," she says to him. "Mine, neither. Come on, let's get a drink."

He follows the Snow Queen to the lemonade table like a dejected puppy, Carleen and Jen in tow.

"Moron," says a voice behind me.

"That's no way to talk about your own cousin," I say, turning to meet Ryan's unsmiling face. I'm surprised to see how close he is. But my parents are waving to me, and I bolt, glad to have an escape, angry at myself for leaving.

Mom and Dad meet me under the shade of an elm tree. Mom's blue eyes never stop moving. She doesn't have her contact lenses in and probably can't see very well. Dad hands me some lemonade and gushes over the contents of the envelope and the certificate.

"This is going on the piano! We're so proud of you," he says, kissing my cheek. "I was always good at math, too. It must be in the genes. Listen, your mom's getting anxious. I'm going to take her home. Would you like me to pick you up later?" He looks at the sky. Thunderheads loom on the horizon. "It looks like rain ..."

"No. I'll get a ride with Marissa's dad." I smile as brightly as possible. "But I'll call you if I need you."

Mom starts to cry. Big tears run slowly down her cheeks. Dad fishes about in his pocket for a tissue. He tries to dab her eyes but she bats his hands away. He traps the fingers of one of her hands, but his attempt to soothe her fails. People are staring.

"Mom, Mom, it's okay. Please, don't cry. Shhh."
I push at Dad until he lets her go. Then I take her
in my arms and hold her for a long time. Her tears
fall, hot and wet, on my neck. Part of me wonders
if they will stain my dress.

Eventually, she stops sobbing. Her face is red and
streaked. Her eyes are so sad, so confused. I should
go home, now, with her. I don't think she'll let Dad
look after her. But she *has* to be all right. Just for
tonight.

As we walk to the car, I reach deep down inside
and find a grin. "I won't be late, Mom. I promise.
Let Dad take you home and fix you supper. Then
you can beat him at crazy eights."

Her shoulders and head droop, like the pansies on
a hot, dry day when they've run out of moisture. She
gets into the car without saying anything. Everything
is blurry with my tears as they drive away.

"Are you okay?" says Ryan. Again he's behind me.

I turn on him. "Will you quit sneaking up
behind me?"

"I'm not sneaking up. I wondered if you needed
some help."

"No, I don't. Every time I see you I think about
my mom having Alzheimer. And I don't want her to
have Alzheimer. All you do is remind me that she's
sick. I ..."

As soon as the words are out, I'm angry at myself again. It's not his fault I'm so emotional. It's not his fault my mom is sick.

"Sylvie, I'm sorry," Ryan says, brushing away one of my tears with his thumb.

"Leave me alone." I don't stop running until I'm in the stuffy gloom of the girls' washroom in the farthest corner of the school.

Chapter Twenty-Five

Marissa pushes open the cubicle door and coaxes me out.

"Do you want to go home?" she asks. "My dad is still here …"

"No, I don't want to go home." I almost shout at her. "I'll be fine."

"Do you want to talk about it? Is Ryan bugging you?"

"Yes, he's bugging me." Then I shake my head. "No, he's not. It's not his fault. I don't want to get into it right now."

She watches while I splash tepid water over my face. I don't care if my dress gets wet marks now. I blow my nose, hard, stalling for time.

"What a pair, eh?" Marissa says, turning her head for a good look in the mirror and touching the fading bruise marks. "Who'd have thought it – you and me, in the bathroom on prom night? It sucks."

"Big time."

"Okay, Sylvie, you don't want to get into it, but I think Ryan only wants to help." She smiles at my reflection. "I think he likes you."

I frown at her suggestion and at the mirror. "Look at me. I'm a mess."

She hands me her eyeliner and mascara. Somehow I make myself presentable.

"Okay. Party time."

"You sure about this?"

I swing open the door. "Absolutely."

As we walk through the dimly lit hallway, I find myself looking for Ryan. I'll apologize, get it over with and then have some fun. I don't see him but I do see Trent, leaning against the wall.

"Bonsoir, mademoiselles. I'm de maitre d'," he says in a terrible French accent. "Dis way to de table especially pour vous."

His seat is, of course, between Cassie and Carleen. Royce and Marissa and I sit with Jen at the other end of the table. Dinner is fried chicken, coleslaw and fries. Not my first choice for a special occasion — but oh well. I pick up my plastic fork and start on the fries.

Trent tells a story about going to the waterslides and some fat old lady losing her bathing suit. Royce and Marissa carry on their own quiet conversation.

Jen is her usual silent self. I guess she only talks at the store. I stare at the blue and silver stars hanging from the rafters, each star bearing the name of a graduating student. Mine is over the dance floor. Ryan is at a table in the corner, laughing with a couple of other guys. He looks at me briefly before attacking his coleslaw.

Before long the tables are littered with chicken bones, bits of french fries and empty salad containers. Trent has lined up the drink cans and cups and is working on a pyramid until Mr. Sisson and Mr. Gregory come along with the recycling box and a garbage bag. The table is cleared by one sweep of Trent's arm.

Butterflies gather in my stomach as soon as the clean-up is finished and the lights go down. I close my eyes tight and make a wish that Trent asks me to dance. He has to – he's my only possibility. Not Royce. Not any of the other jocks who've never so much as spoken to me. And certainly not Ryan.

So I sit. And I wait. And the night wears on and I sit, go to the bathroom, come back and sit. I polish off a plate of pretzels and pretend to enjoy watching Marissa and Royce. My heart stops when Ryan walks over. I don't look at him in case he can tell I'm holding my breath.

He asks Carleen and then Jen. They refuse. He

walks off. I'm stunned, but what did I expect? It's my own stupid fault.

Trent is talking to one of the teachers. Cassie, Jen and Carleen never leave the table. Their eyes never leave the dance floor. Out of sheer boredom, I sit beside Cassie.

"Having fun yet?" Her tone is cold and haughty.

"How come you're not dancing?"

"Trent doesn't dance. Doesn't know how," she answers with a flip of her long pale hair. "Dancing's for nerds, right?"

Jen and Carleen nod. Trent doesn't dance! There must be an awful lot of nerds in the world — and some of them are in the school hall. I go back to my own seat.

In my mind I see my mom and dad dancing. It was at a wedding, years ago. I remember how great they looked together. Mom used to say that a man who couldn't or wouldn't dance was afraid of looking stupid. Mom used to say a lot of things.

I might as well go home. I'll play cards if Mom is still up. Maybe Dad and I can have a real game. Maybe there's a good movie on TV.

"Cassie, would you like to dance?"

Ryan has his hand out, but the Snow Queen sniffs. "Dancing is for nerds," she repeats. "Why don't you ask Queen Nerd of the Study Hall over there?"

It takes a second for it to sink in that I'm Queen Nerd. Ryan sits next to me.

"So, do you wanna dance? Or are you still mad and want me to leave you alone?"

My mind goes numb. The deejay plays a waltz. Don't think. Just do it!

Ryan takes my hand and leads me to the spot on the floor under my star. The warmth of his body, the strength of his arm around my waist — I want to tell him that I really do appreciate his trying to help me, but I don't have the words. I get the feeling he could become a good friend. When the music stops, he asks me if I want to dance again.

I gather my courage, raise my face to Ryan's and dazzle him with my smile. He swallows and his Adam's apple goes up and down. He seems to be gathering courage, too.

"About what my grandmother said, last winter. In the park ... about us ..."

My heart does a backflip. "That's all right," I say. "I understand now."

"It was still really embarrassing." He chuckles nervously. "I mean, I hardly knew you. Sometimes she says strange things like that. Maybe she knows something we don't." A moment of heavy silence. "You look very beautiful, Sylvie."

"Thank you," I reply in my best grown-up voice.

"I wasn't ignoring you all night," he adds hurriedly. "But you told me to leave you alone."

"I know. I'm sorry. Besides, being Queen Nerd of the Study Hall is okay when it means getting awards and getting to dance."

His fingers tighten around my hand.

Chapter Twenty-Six

The rain pelts the windshield. The wipers can hardly keep up. Eye-searing lightning slashes the black night, and the thunder seems to roll over the roof of Mr. Plummer's car. In the front seat, Marissa is telling her father all about the fantastic time she had with Royce and how she wished his mother hadn't come to take him home so early. Mr. Plummer is trying to pay attention to what she is saying, but he is focused on driving. When we pull up to the entrance of my block, he makes to get out and walk me in, but I tell him no.

As soon as I step into the parking lot, I'm soaked. The wind tears at my hair and stings my eyes. My dress is a soggy rag by the time I reach the foyer. The face in the elevator mirror is tired and pale but happy.

I dance my way down the silent hallway to our apartment. The place is in semidarkness. Only the light over the kitchen table is on low. It's like walking into the past, when all was peaceful and everyone was where they should be and everything was as it should be. Then I hear irregular snoring and the droning of late-night TV. Probably Dad, asleep on the couch. Quietly, I tiptoe to my room, strip off my soaking-wet dress and put on my nightie.

I decide to wait awhile before waking him. I pad to Mom's room – just to look in on her. Maybe, just maybe, she'll be her old self. Slowly, I open the door. The night-light on her dresser is glowing orange. Her room is more of a mess than usual, if that's possible – the duvet one big roll in the middle of the bed.

"Mom," I say in a loud whisper. "Mom, are you awake?"

I reach to peek into the comforter, expecting to find my mother's wary eyes darting around. I prepare myself to soothe her fear. The blanket unrolls easily.

She's not there.

I can't handle this. Not tonight. I check the hall closet and the broom closet in case Mom is hiding, but I know in my heart it's useless.

Trying very hard to control my temper and my fear, I march into the living room and shake the sleeping beauty wrapped in my afghan. "Wake up. Wake up!"

"What's that?"

"Mrs. Rathbone? What are *you* doing here?"

She rocks herself up off the couch. "Your dad got called away. Some emergency at his job site."

"Mom's gone! What happened? Where'd she go?"

"Gone? I ... I ... don't know. When I got here she was ready for bed. Your dad had made them supper, and Marianne seemed all right when he left."

"And then? Come on. Think. Please! Did anything go wrong? Did anything upset her?"

"Oh, it's this damn cold medication. It makes me so sleepy," Mrs. Rathbone whimpers. "She was sitting at that table playing hand after hand of solitaire. You know, you can't actually *play* with her, so I lay down on the couch. I guess I drifted off ..."

"I guess!" I run my hand through my wet hair. "She wouldn't have gone outside, would she?"

She shrugs. "I don't know, dear."

"She hates bad storms. Hates to see people out in them. Did she talk at all? How long have you been asleep?" My voice is getting very loud.

Mrs. Rathbone rubs her forehead. "Last time I looked at the clock it was around ten-thirty. Oh dear — two hours ago. I'm sorry. I really am. Maybe I'm getting too old ... too old to be of use." Her eyes fill with tears.

"Oh, don't start crying, for heaven's sake," I say with less sympathy than she deserves.

"Sylvie dear, maybe we should call the police."

"Not yet." I peer out the window just as Mom might have done earlier this evening. What would she see in this rain? Streetlights glow on the bridge, and the lamps below our apartment give off a muted yellow halo. The trees bend under the force of the wind. She was probably waiting for me to come home.

"I bet she tried to find me," I mutter. "When the storm began, Mrs. Rathbone, what was she wearing?"

"Her white housecoat. Call your father."

I press the speed-dial button on the telephone and hang up when his answering machine clicks in.

I take Mrs. Rathbone by the shoulders. "Stay here. In case she comes back."

I grab my denim jacket and swing it over my nightie. "I'm going to check the building and maybe outside."

She clutches at my sleeve. "Are you sure that's —"

"Wait here." I fly down flight after flight of stairs and hallway after carpeted hallway. There are so many places to hide, but I don't think she wants to hide. I think she's looking for me. I push back the rising panic and take the elevator to the main floor.

I come to the back hallway. The door is self locking. One shove on the crash bar and I'm outside. The rain drives in sheets against the building. I shield my eyes.

"Mom! Mom!"

The wind howls like a hundred ghosts. I can see nothing but the cowering trees. I am about to step out into the wild night when a movement along the wall catches my eye. A person is plastered into a corner. Its lips are moving in some silent conversation.

"Mom!" I scream. "Mom!"

She hears me but doesn't reply. I can't go to her. We'd be locked out.

"Mom, it's me, Sylvie. Daughter. Come inside. It's all right now."

Gradually a smile overtakes her terrified expression and she runs into my arms. The storm slams the door shut, sending a furious rain against it.

Mom is laughing. It's been so long since I heard her laugh. I believe she is happy to see me and relieved that I'm not hurt.

I wipe her wet face gently with the sleeve of my jacket. "You were worried about me. You haven't forgotten me."

Dad's words spring up, about her being unable

to get her mind around what her heart is feeling. A huge lump is stuck in my throat as I half carry her back to a nearly hysterical Mrs. Rathbone hovering in our living room.

"You found her." Mrs. Rathbone immediately takes off Mom's wet housecoat and slippers. "Where was she?"

"At the back door."

"Here, let me help you get her into a nice warm tub." Mrs Rathbone starts ushering Mom to the bathroom.

"Please, Mrs. Rathbone." I hold up my hand to stop her. "You've done enough."

"Haven't I just." Her eyes are brimming again.

"I didn't mean it like that." I give her a quick hug. "I mean, you spent all evening with her when you're not well, and it's so late. Why not get some rest? Sleep in tomorrow."

"I always sleep in," she sniffs and then regains her composure. "You are right, dear. I'm very tired. But can you manage?"

"I can manage," I assure her. "And thank you for being so nice to us — especially these last few weeks. I know you won't take any money, but why don't you come over for supper? You pick the day. I'll cook us something special."

"That's very nice of you, dear, after the way I

messed up tonight."

"Couldn't be helped." I give her another hug. "Go to bed. Good night."

"Good night, both of you," she says sadly.

I look away while Mom has her shower and as I help her on with her pajamas. She sits calmly on the closed toilet lid as I blow-dry her hair.

"Come on, Mom," I say, working our way to my bedroom. "You get to sleep by the wall."

She seems happy to share my bed and falls asleep instantly. I snuggle against her in the spoon position I used to love so much when I was little and listen to the thunder rolling away into the distance. The rain is lighter now but the wind still rattles the window.

Another fear shakes me. Alzheimer can be hereditary — maybe I've got it. Maybe I shouldn't have kids. Who will look after *me*?

I shudder and hold on tighter to Mom.

Chapter Twenty-Seven

I dream I'm being rained on. When I wake I realize it's not totally a dream. The bed and my nightie are wet! And the smell! Grossed out, I roll onto the floor and peer under the covers. Mom is still sawing logs. A large irregular circle of darkened sheet surrounds her lower body. She peed my bed!

It is at that moment I realize I won't be able to look after her myself for long. For now, I guess I'm going to have to buy some of the adult diapers I see advertised on TV. I hate the idea.

There's no point waking her up. The damage has been done. I stomp to the bathroom to clean myself up and then pull on a pair of white cotton shorts and my save the whales sweatshirt that's the same as Marissa's.

I think about phoning Dad, but when the dome clock on the piano chimes nine, I realize he will be on his way over. I plug in the kettle, stick two pieces of bread in the toaster and step onto the balcony. The intense heat and humidity blast me. The pansies are struggling to stand straight after the pounding of the storm last night. Broken branches and pieces of paper are strewn on the back parking lot and the grass. One of the trees near the river has split jaggedly in half. But there is no wind today, no breeze, and the air is stifling.

I go into the living room and dial Marissa's number.

"You'll never believe what happened last night when I got home," I say as soon as she answers. She listens without interruption as I tell her about Mom going missing. "I was *so* terrified. She could've been anywhere."

Marissa sighs. "We need to get together. How about we take my wonder siblings to the park for a picnic soon."

"Good idea. How are you?"

"Fine," she says.

"Hey, I say I'm fine all the time, especially when I'm not."

"But I am *fine*. Not fantastic. Not great. Not terrible. Just fine. Fine is Royce. We had such a great time. He wants to take me to a movie."

Almost afraid to ask, I change the subject. "How is Jasper?"

She takes a while to answer. "He's coming along. He's so clingy."

"What about your dad?"

"He's working so hard at this family stuff. He takes time to talk to each kid before he tucks them into bed. Before, he would hardly have a thing to say. I guess he was so angry at Mom, with her moods and all. Jasper will sit on his knee now — he wouldn't before. I don't know what's going to happen after Dad uses up his holiday time. He'll need to get a different job so he can stay in the city. My Aunt Sarah is here for a while but she can't stay forever."

"Well, I'm here for you ... if you need me, Marissa," I say, swallowing the sudden build-up of emotion. "I am, you know."

"Me too, old pal. How's it going with your father?"

"Not bad. I guess I'm gonna have to live with him." I sigh. "I don't know how much longer I can look after Mom."

"Funny how things work out," she says carefully.

We hang up just as Mom shows her face in the kitchen. I throw the wet sheets into the laundry hamper and get her to help me put on fresh ones. She follows me around as if afraid she might lose me, which is fine — that means she won't take off again.

Dad arrives carrying a brown bag overflowing with groceries. "Hi, Marianne. Hi, Sylvie. How was the dance?"

I'm amazed at how relieved, and pleased, I am that he's here. Leaving Mom to channel surf, I haul him into my bedroom so she won't hear.

"When I came home last night, you were gone, Mrs. Rathbone was snoring on the couch, and Mom was missing. I found her out back of the building, but I thought I was going to have a heart attack, I was so scared."

"Oh, Sylvie." He crushes me in a tight squeeze.

I surprise us both by saying, "Dad, please move back. I need you here."

Chapter Twenty-Eight

Four days later, I sit in Dr. Gina's office, yawning widely to suck in the cool air.

Dr. Gina's eyes narrow but she says nothing. A lady is talking to Mom, assessing her, trying to find out how far gone she is, I guess.

"Mrs. Marchione, do you know your doctor's name?"

"Dr. Gina," answers Mom. I yawn again.

"And this lovely young woman?"

"Sylvie!"

My yawn halts halfway. She's here! Mom's plugged in!

"Do you know who I am and why I'm here?"

Mom gives Joan the once-over, taking in her beige suit and printed scarf, intelligent, soft brown eyes and hair and sallow complexion.

"Joan Frazer. I'm with the Alzheimer Society."

The brightness in Mom's face dims. "Ah, I understand."

"Do you, Mrs. Marchione?" asks Joan. "Do you understand that you are not well?"

"Yes!" Mom snaps.

Joan touches Mom's arm. "From what Sylvie says, you have been sleeping during the days and walking around at nights."

Mom frowns.

"Your daughter is becoming run down. She's yawned at least ten times since we started this meeting."

"I'm sorry." I blush.

"You have nothing to be sorry for, dear," she replies. "Mrs. Marchione, Sylvie – I would like you and your family to consider coming to one of our day programs if possible or at least to sit in on a support group." She pauses. "When Dr. Gina asked me to come here today, I hesitated. We prefer to wait until the family contacts us. That way there is no sense of the family being pressured. But, because you are so young, Marianne, and are declining so rapidly, I agreed to meet you. I think it is important that you both know what services are available, and that you are not alone." She flicks me a sympathetic glance. "Arrangements will soon need to be made for a nursing home –"

"No!" I jump up and cross my arms. "No nursing home, no hospital."

Joan puts her arm around me and lowers me into my chair. "Dear, you need to plan —"

"No!" I stick out my chin. "Dad has moved in. We can look after her!"

"Oh, Sylvie," sighs Mom.

"Have you made any legal arrangements?" asks Dr. Gina.

Mom nods. Her head is drooping like one of the sun-wilted pansies on our balcony.

"Is there a living will?" asks Joan.

"A what?" I squeak.

Dr. Gina picks up my question. "A living will comes into effect when the patient has a nine-nine and —"

"Nine-nine? What's that?"

"It's a hospital code to indicate a patient who is having a heart attack. Then the responding team brings the crash cart — like on those television medical dramas." She looks past me. "A living will states that this particular patient does not want the crash cart or heroic measures to be taken to save her life."

I gasp. "She'll die! Besides she's not going to need lifesaving measures. Tell them, Mom!"

All three women lower their eyes.

"No, not at the moment," says Dr. Gina. "But in a progressive dementing illness such as Alzheimer the nervous system fails as well. The body is severely affected, causing pneumonia, dehydration, stroke —"

"Okay, okay," I interrupt, "but this doesn't happen for years and years, right?"

"Not necessarily, dear," answers Joan. "Now, I haven't had a lot of experience explaining Alzheimer to a teenager. Usually, caregivers are middle-aged children or spouses. But about the support groups. We meet every —"

"Thank you. I've read the brochure." I pull Mom to her feet. Tears are coursing down her cheeks. "Look what you've done — she's crying. Oh, Mom, don't cry. Come on, let's go home."

"Sylvie, please," says Dr. Gina. "Don't go."

But Joan steps between us. "Sylvie's right, Dr. Caswell. She has the brochure and can reach us anytime. It's a pleasure to meet you."

She extends her hand. Mom shakes it. I open the door and storm out with Mom at my heels.

"I don't need to hear all that depressing stuff," I cry. "Neither do you."

"We'll have to deal with it."

"What's this *we* bit. You will be in la-la land by then. I'll have to deal with it. And I'm not ready, at this very second."

"Have to deal with them!"

"You know something, Mom? I'm beginning to wish you didn't have these little moments of ... what's it called ... lucidity? I think I like it better when you just sit there playing solitaire by your own stupid rules. And, while you're *here*, there's a few other things I'd like to get cleared up."

In the taxi, I try to talk about Dad, but she says she's too tired. So, we're silent, but the argument starts as soon as we reach the apartment block.

"Why wouldn't you let me see Dad?"

She pulls herself up straight. "I let you see him."

"He says you didn't tell me when he called and left him waiting when you'd arranged visits. He says that you made it all up about him being too busy to see me."

She grows sullen. "He said that, did he?"

"That's his side of the story. What's yours?"

"We stopped getting along," she answers simply. "I did what I thought was best for all of us."

"No, you did what you thought was best for you!" I growl. "And all this time I blamed everything on Dad. Why did you let me? Why did you lie? I think you knew you were going crazy ... and ... oh, never mind."

Mouth open, she stares at me. Before she can reply, I turn and leave her standing there in the foyer. I march into the dazzling afternoon and over the bridge to the park. If she's so damned "together," she can get herself up to the apartment.

The park is packed with teenagers, walkers, joggers and skateboarders. Luckily, I don't meet anyone I know, and with no one to feed into my anger, it eventually fades.

It's not her fault, my guilty conscience reminds me, and I march back out of the park and head for home. It's not like Mom did something to cause this illness. It's not anybody's fault. There's no one to blame. I wish there was. It would make things easier.

I pause for a moment on the crest of the bridge. Not one cloud interrupts the vast blue sky. Speedboats and canoes pass one another as the Red River sweeps north. Across the concrete parking lot, I can see our apartment windows clearly. The sun makes the sliding door gleam like the gold locket in my jewelry box.

I cover the remaining distance quickly. All the way up in the elevator, I rehearse my apologies, hoping she will forgive me.

The door to our apartment is locked. She's shut me out. I don't blame her. I use my key.

"I'm sorry, Mom, really I am ..." She's not in the kitchen. I do a quick search of the apartment, including closets, under the beds and the foldout couch in

Ishbel Moore

the living room. The terrifying reality sets in.

She never found her way from the foyer — I upset her so much by arguing, she got unplugged.

I bang on Mrs. Rathbone's door.

"Are you in there? Open up!" I holler. "Is Mom in there? Mrs. Rathbone?"

There's no answer.

Okay. Don't panic. Check the building and the grounds. I scour every floor and open area. The hair salon and store are closed. She's not in the parking lot. The pathway is alive with people walking their dogs. The track along the riverbank reveals nothing but bicycle tracks and footprints. Shaking and out of breath, I return to the apartment.

What to do? I phone Dad. His secretary tells me he's not there but she'll try to find him. Marissa will be busy with the kids now that her dad is out of town again. I can't call the police — if they find her, they might turn her over to some institution.

Think, Sylvie, think!

I spy the Alzheimer book on the piano. Ryan! His phone number is on the first page.

My fingers won't dial properly. They keep hitting the wrong buttons. I try three times before I get through.

"Mrs. Kostelniuk? This is Sylvie Marchione."

"Sylvie, is something wrong? Your voice is shaking."

"Is Ryan home, please?"

"Yes, just a moment."

I pace until I hear his voice.

"It's Mom." The tears start and my voice gets higher and higher. "I don't know where she is."

"Calm down, Sylvie," he says. "You're sure she's not with a neighbor?"

"I've checked everywhere! She's not in the building. She's not on the grounds. We had a big argument and …" A sob bursts from my chest and I can't finish.

"Stay where you are. I'll be right over. Try to think about where she might go. But don't go on your own. Wait for me!"

I listen to the dial tone. He's on his way! Thank you, Ryan.

Chapter Twenty-Nine

I perch on the edge of the piano bench, biting my lip. When the buzzer sounds – finally – I jump to my feet, hitting the piano with my thigh. It's a bruising pain but I hardly notice.

"I'll be right down," I cry into the intercom.

He's drumming his fingers on the roof of the white car, but he stops as I run toward him.

"Oh, Ryan. I thought you'd never get here."

"I brought my mom."

Mrs. Kostelniuk leans out the car window. "Where are we going? Any ideas?"

I shrug. "The only thing I can think of is that maybe she tried to follow me to Kildonan Park, and somehow I missed her and she got lost."

"What mood was she in?" Mrs. Kostelniuk's face is pinched with worry.

"It's hard to say. When I left her in the foyer, she was her old self. Lucid, you know, talking like you and me. We had a big fight. I yelled at her and then walked away. I don't know after that."

"The changes happen so quickly sometimes. Let's go to the park."

"What is she wearing?" Ryan asks as we fold ourselves into the little car.

"A long brown skirt and a white T-shirt with gold pyramids on the front. Listen, I really appreciate this." I can't look at him. I keep scanning out the window.

"No problem," says Mrs. Kostelniuk. "I hope we find her before dark, that's all."

"If this was winter she could be frozen to death in a snowbank by now," I cry. "Some maniac could hurt her and leave her to die in some field ..."

"Stop it, Sylvie," Ryan says gently. "You'll go crazy thinking like that."

Ryan reaches back for my hand. He curls his strong fingers around my trembling ones.

"I can't help it." I sniff and wipe my free hand across my nose. "What if she's scared? What if she's so scared she tries to kill herself again?"

Mrs. Kostelniuk's eyes meet mine in the rearview mirror. "She's tried to kill herself?"

"I ... I'm not sure. I think so. What if she throws herself in front of a bus. Into the river?"

"Sylvie, cut it out!" Ryan orders.

"I love her," I sob. "I don't want to lose her. I don't want her to die or spend the rest of her life unable to think. I want my mom back!"

He hands me a tissue from the box on the dash.

I blow my nose noisily. "Sorry."

"Don't be sorry. Just let's find your mom."

We start around the big loop of park road close to the river, past the outdoor theater, the big field where churches hold their picnics, and past the creek, the pavilion, the swimming pool and the English Gardens. My heart clenches with agony each time I see a blonde head or a white T-shirt.

Mrs. Kostelniuk cranes her neck as she peers from the car. "We'd need a search party to walk the monkey trails and the treed parts. Are you sure there's nowhere else you can think of? Is there anywhere that you went recently where you had fun or spent any length of time together that was pleasant?"

I push the cold dread from my terrified brain and try to think. I come up empty. "We go every-where together – and nowhere."

"Then, I'll tell you what," she says. "Let's go back and drive the streets close to your apartment block for an hour. If we have no luck, Sylvie, we will have to phone the police."

I nod.

We cross the bridge in the lengthening shadows and stop for the red light at Henderson. The market garden is open and people are milling about. Some instinct makes me cry out.

"Try in there! We bought flowers here the other week. We won a prize, a trowel, for being the one-hundredth customer. Maybe she's there."

Ryan's mother pulls onto the gravel parking lot. We leap from the car and head into the bright blossom-filled hothouses. The small aisles are crowded with men and women sweating in the humidity and still air. My shorts and tank top stick to me. Ryan's forehead is glistening when we leave.

The garden-accessories and trees sections are not so busy, but Mom is not there. We excuse ourselves over and over again as we push our way around the annuals and perennials.

I spot her deadheading petunias. Relief makes my knees weak – I think I'm going to collapse.

"Mom! Mom!" I cry, but she doesn't hear me. An attendant comes to my side.

"Do you know that woman?"

"She's my mother. I've been looking all over for her."

"I'm glad you're here. We're getting ready to close, and she's running out of petunias to prune." She smiles and her sunbeaten skin wrinkles around her eyes and mouth.

Ishbel Moore

"Thank you for being so patient with her."

Ryan prods me forward but doesn't come with me. Instead he and his mother go back to the car.

"Mom?" I approach her slowly.

She turns and raises her hand to block out the sun's rays. Her face is blank, her eyes empty.

She cocks her head to one side. She doesn't recognize me. I could be anybody. I could be an ax murderer. Petunia petals float to the ground.

"Come on, Mom! It's me, Sylvie. Daughter."

She allows me to guide her to the car.

Chapter Thirty

Mom sits in the big leather chair and stares out of the dim hospital-room window, across the dark prairies stretching north. She's hardly spoken in the last three hours except for single words that have nothing to do with what's happening.

Dad keeps shaking his head and sighing. His secretary never gave up trying to reach him, and he arrived at the hospital shortly after we did.

"This *is* the right thing to do," Dr. Gina says. "I'm going to keep Marianne here for a day or two. After a thorough assessment we'll know what to do next."

"I can't think of next. That's why we brought her here," I say wearily. "I'm wrecked. All I've done is cry."

"It's perfectly understandable." She smiles. "I know how strongly you feel about not having her placed in a nursing home."

"I don't even want to talk about it."

"But, do you see — it would eventually become impossible for you. Even if you watch her every waking — and sleeping — moment, you will never be able to keep it up." She pats my hand. "This may sound unkind, Sylvie, but the person you searched for tonight is not your mother. She's gone, dear. She doesn't know where she is or who we are."

"Not always," I argue.

"Those moments will get more and more rare. And I understand she's incontinent at night now as well. You have to let go." She pats my hand again to show her concern and support. "Go home now. Try to get some rest. Your mom is in good hands." Her words, however kind and gentle, end the conversation.

I kiss Mom on the cheek. "I'm going now." I wait for a reaction. Nothing. "I'll come visit you tomorrow." Still nothing. "Good night, Mom."

Dad slips my arm through his. "Come on, honey. Let's go."

I pause at the doorway for one last glance at my beautiful, talented mother. She suddenly twists in the chair and looks at me. For a moment, something like recognition flickers in her eyes, then dies, and she turns back to the window. I hear Dad's sharp intake of breath, and I know he saw it and felt it, too.

Ryan falls in behind as we walk through the quiet ward. He's been here the whole time, since his mother dropped us off at the emergency entrance.

With each step, my mind fills with a different memory. Mom beating Marissa and me at five-thousand rummy while the sun sets over the lake. Mom whipping up her latest gourmet creation while I practice piano. Mom totally engrossed in the ballet, the stage lights illuminating her lovely face. Mom and I sitting on the balcony, talking — about the weather, the river, anything. Mom on the balcony, ready to let go of that hanging basket.

Dad pulls out of the parking lot, away from the hospital, away from Mom. The three of us, Dad, Ryan and me, are lost in our thoughts. No one speaks until we turn onto the bridge.

"Where do you live, Ryan?" Dad asks. "I'll drop you off. It's the least I can do. I'll ... we'll always be grateful to you and your mother."

"Our house is only one street over from your building. I can walk. In fact, I wanna walk."

"Suit yourself." Dad looks at Ryan's reflection in the rearview mirror. "But come by any time you like. You'll always be welcome." Ryan mumbles his thanks.

Dad parks in the lot, and I haul myself out of the car. The night air is cool on my hot face. Dad shakes

Ryan's hand. "You've been very kind, but we're quite all right now, aren't we, Sylvie?"

"Actually, Dad, I'd like to talk to Ryan. I'll meet you upstairs."

"Are you sure? It's very late."

"I'm sure."

We don't move until he enters the building and the elevator doors close behind him. I send Ryan a shy smile.

"Thanks for everything. Your mother is nice. Same as you. The way she took control when we got back to the apartment — calling the doctor, packing Mom's things, letting Dad's office know where we'd be — and all I could do was rock like a baby and cry. She must think I'm a total twit."

"I doubt it." He smiles. "But I really should go. You've had a very hard day."

"No." I reach for him. "Don't go yet."

He hesitates, then we turn and head along the brightly lit pathway that circles the apartment block. We go quite far before I break the silence.

"Do we have it? Alzheimer?" I blurt out. "Will I get like my mom? What about my kids if I have any? And their kids? Maybe people like me and you shouldn't have kids. Break the cycle."

He stops and shakes his head. "I dunno. Scary, isn't it?"

"But you know so much about it," I say. "I thought you'd know."

"Some get it, some don't," he answers flatly. "My parents are okay, so far. But Dad's worried. Grandma wasn't always like she is now. One day she's teaching me chess. Next day she doesn't know the difference between the king and a pawn! I got so mad at her. Now I understand better. But it scares me." He takes a deep breath and looks away.

We wander along until we come to the river. The water is dark and moving quickly. The trees rustle in the breeze.

"So, what are you gonna do now?" he asks.

I try to keep my voice even, but it cracks anyway. "I guess I've got to grow up." His arms wrap around me – strong and gentle. I can feel his heart pounding against my cheek. "I'm glad you moved to Winnipeg."

"Me too," he whispers. "I'm getting attached to the place. How's about you and me go to a movie – when you're ready."

A tiny flame spurts in my heart and I nod.

He holds my hand and walks me back to the door.

"I'd better get going." He smiles and I feel the tears welling again. "Don't cry," he says. "I'll call you tomorrow. Try to get some sleep, okay?"

"Okay," I whisper. "Good night."

He takes several backward steps, waves and then starts running. I watch as he moves from bright to dark to bright beneath the streetlights.

I study my face in the mirror as the elevator rises to the tenth floor. I look terrible, mascara streaks partly wiped off, eyes watery, skin pale. I walk slowly down the long hallway and into our apartment. The door closes behind me with a soft click.

Dad is on the balcony. My heart leaps with remembered terror and I rush across the room. But both his feet are firmly on the cement and his hands are fiercely gripping the railing. Tears stream down his cheeks. My breathing returns to normal.

I lean my head against his shoulder and stare up at the night sky.